a coyote's in the house

elmore leonard

illustrated by lauren child

PUFFIN

PUFFIN BOOKS

Published by the Penguin Group
Penguin Books Ltd, 80 Strand, London WC2R ORL, England
Penguin Group (USA) Inc., 375 Hudson Street, New York, New York 10014, USA
Penguin Books Australia Ltd, 250 Camberwell Road, Camberwell, Victoria 3124, Australia
Penguin Books Canada Ltd, 10 Alcorn Avenue, Toronto, Ontario, Canada M4V 3B2
Penguin Books India (P) Ltd, 11 Community Centre, Panchsheel Park, New Delhi – 110 017, India
Penguin Group (NZ), cnr Airborne and Rosedale Roads, Albany, Auckland 1310, New Zealand
Penguin Books (South Africa) (Pty) Ltd, 24 Sturdee Avenue, Rosebank 2196, South Africa

Penguin Books Ltd, Registered Offices: 80 Strand, London WC2R ORL, England

www.penguin.com

First published in the United States of America by HarperCollins Books 2004
Published in Great Britain in hardback in Puffin Books 2004
Published in paperback 2005

1

Text copyright © Elmore Leonard, 2004
Illustrations copyright © Lauren Child, 2004
All rights reserved

The moral right of the author and illustrator has been asserted

Set in Monotype Baskerville
Typeset by Rowland Phototypesetting Ltd, Bury St Edmunds, Suffolk
Made and printed in England by Clays Ltd, St Ives plc

British Library Cataloguing in Publication Data
A CIP catalogue record for this book is available from the British Library

ISBN 0-141-31688-8

For my grandchildren: Shannon and Megan; Tim, Alex, Max and Kate; Ben, Hillary and Abby; Joe, Nick and Luke; and for my great-grandson, Jack.

one

Here was Antwan, living the life of a young coyote up in the Hollywood Hills, loving it, but careful to keep out of the way of humans.

Humans were crazy. Some would feed you, some would shoot at you for no reason. Yell at coyotes, 'Go on back where you came from.' But this *was* where they came from. They had lived in these hills the past forty thousand years or so.

It was their turf.

All Antwan and his gang wanted to do was hang with the pack, goof around, groom each other for ticks and fleas, flirt with the sisters and mostly chase after whatever kinds of creatures were out of their holes. Mice were the most fun, 'cause you could play with 'em before you ate 'em.

Mice ate crickets and crunchy bugs, and coyotes ate mice. It wasn't to be mean or cruel. It was what the law of nature told you to do if you were a coyote. The same as when they went after possums and raccoons, or rabbits hippity-hopping down the bunny trail. Even kitty cats and little doggies humans kept as pets, they were all on the coyote food list, okay to eat.

Understand, if the mice or other creatures were hiding out in their holes or off looking for food, then Antwan and his gang would have to go looking for it, too.

Go to where humans lived, down back of their houses where they kept their trash cans. It was dangerous 'cause you had to look out for humans. Some even tried to run over you with their cars. But if they didn't build their houses right here, Antwan and his gang wouldn't be going through their garbage.

Antwan was the leader of the gang, known as the Howling Diablos, because he was the smartest and the fastest of all the young coyotes. The Diablos were pretty sure that in time, say in a year or so, Antwan would be the one to tussle with Cletus, the pack leader, and run the old dude off. Then Antwan would be the head of the whole pack and have his pick of the bitches. He'd choose the one he'd like to hang with the rest of his life and have his pups.

Right now Antwan was busy looking after his little sister, Ramona, seeing she didn't get in trouble. Ramona was dying to join the Diablos, but hadn't yet learned enough about life in the wild to run with the big boys.

Antwan was teaching her.

Saturday afternoons he'd take Ramona to a dog park over in another part of the hills, a good place to show his sister the different breeds of dogs there were in the world, the ones easy to snatch and eat and the ones you didn't want to mess with. Antwan and Ramona would crouch in the bushes, up on the side of the canyon, and look down at the humans and their pets, some coming up the mile-long trail from Hollywood, while others were walking down: all kinds of dogs passing both ways. It was like a show.

'Here comes a working dog, a Border collie,' Antwan said, 'only he's out of work. Rides around Hollywood in his owner's car looking for sheep to herd.'

'I know what collies look like,' Ramona said. 'They have that long, pointy face.'

'Other dogs do, too,' Antwan said. 'Your borzois, your Afghan hounds . . . What's that white one coming?'

'A greyhound?'

'You're close, but it's a saluki.'

'What's it do?'

'Lays around the house thinking it's somebody.'

Ramona said, 'I know greyhounds chase rabbits.'

'Yeah, toy ones,' Antwan said. 'They chase 'em around a racetrack and humans bet money on which one's gonna win.'

Ramona wouldn't know what he was talking about. It took time to learn all the weird things dogs had to do. Antwan said now, 'Here come some more working dogs, like the collie. That black one's a bouvier and the little shorty's a corgi. Put them out on a farm they can't wait to start herding sheep, or even geese. That make sense to you, having to work? It's hard to believe coyotes and dogs are in the same family, dogs having sold out, gone over to the human side. They're more like them than they are us.'

Antwan said now, 'Here comes a hunting dog, a pointer. He points to where the game bird's hiding – like a pheasant, the one with the long tail? And the human shoots the bird as it flies up in the air.'

'So the pointer's like somebody that tattles on you,' Ramona said, 'a snitch?'

'That's right, honey,' Antwan said, 'you're

4

learning your breeds. What's that one with the big floppy ears?'

'A bloodhound.'

'And what's he do?'

'Catches your scent and sniffs after you.'

'That dog's so dumb,' Antwan said, 'he'll track you all day and all night for a treat and a pat on the head. All these dogs, they'll do tricks, sit up and roll over, to get a treat put in their mouth.'

'I never had one,' Ramona said.

'A treat? You haven't missed anything. Okay, what's that dog – you see him down there taking a pee?'

'A German shepherd.'

'Wrong. It's a Siberian husky, tough as they come. He'll sleep outside all night in the snow and pull a sled all day.'

'What's snow?'

'That white stuff you see on top of Mt Wilson.' He waited for Ramona to ask him what a sled was.

But Ramona was looking at a dog with big droopy ears and a long black coat to the ground. She said, 'What's that one?'

'Some kind of spaniel,' Antwan said. 'A human shoots a duck out of the sky, it falls in the lake and that retriever dog swims out and fetches it. Doesn't mind getting wet. Only around here it doesn't do nothing but sleep and get food handed to it.'

Ramona said, 'What's wrong with that?'

And Antwan said, 'Could you lay around all day? Never hunt your own food? Come up here to be shown off? What good would you be, to the pack or to yourself?'

'I could have fun playing,' Ramona said, looking at a boy with a chihuahua jumping up at him, 'like that little one there.'

'You want to be known as a toy?' Antwan said. 'That's all that dog is. There's some more, the Lhasa apso and that lowrider they call a dachshund – looks like a sausage and smells like it, too. They're tasty enough, but give me a rabbit or a half dozen mice for breakfast any day.'

Now Ramona was watching a human throwing a ball to his dog standing above him on the trail, the dog catching the ball in his mouth, then dropping it to roll down the slope to the human. She said, 'Antwan, look how smart that dog is.'

'You mean smart for being a dog, don't you?' Antwan noticed it wore a red bandana tied around its neck. 'Tell me what kind of dog it is.'

'*That* one's a German shepherd.'

'What's it good for, if anything?'

'Guarding places, homes.'

'That's why they call it a police dog. But it can be mean and nasty,' Antwan said, 'though I have

6

my doubts about this one, trying to look stylish with that red hankie.'

'I wouldn't mind having a yellow one,' Ramona said. 'You have to admit it's a smart dog, rolling the ball back to its master.'

'There,' Antwan said. 'You just said the word makes all the difference, "its *master*". The dog's forgot who he is. Thinks he's only supposed to do what his master wants. Tell me you'd rather play catch with that smelly human than run after rabbits.' He watched Ramona begin to nod her head, thinking about it, Antwan hoping the girl wasn't getting the idea dogs were as smart as coyotes, or had anywhere near as much fun in their miserable dog lives.

Antwan's gaze moved down the trail and stopped and right away he began licking his lips. He said to Ramona, 'See the two kids with the show bitch poodle? Cream coloured, tricked out with the puffs and pom-poms? That's what you call gourmet dining.'

After the dog lesson that day Antwan said, 'Come on,' and he and Ramona raced across open slopes, circled homes perched on hillsides, saw a little girl wave from a deck that hung out in the sky; they ducked through gullies, thick brush and stands of trees following trails that only coyotes knew about.

They were in sight of home, the high ravine where the pack lived in caves and crevices and had its dens. Antwan stopped.

He raised his face and heard it again, closer, that *caw caw caw* of a crow, and said, 'It's Cicero, Cicero Crow.'

Ramona wasn't so sure. She said, 'Or is it a flock of 'em spotted us out here?'

Every once in a while she'd hear about crows catching a coyote out in a field by himself. They'd dive on him, peck him to death and clean his bones, leave nothing but his pelt.

'Believe me, it's Cicero,' Antwan said, and saw him in the sky alone, circling, then flying off a couple of times and coming back again until Antwan said, 'Let's go,' and started off in the direction the crow was taking them.

Ramona, running close to Antwan, said, 'I don't know why you trust him.'

'I don't,' Antwan said, 'but we still buddies, help each other out. I know his caw and he knows my howl. I let him know about a roadkill so smelly and squished only a crow or a buzzard would eat it. He tells me where there's a special kind of garbage treat waiting.'

Just then Cicero circled and landed with a hop about ten yards in front of them. He greeted them in his screechy voice saying, 'My man Antwan and his sweet little sister.' He ignored Ramona growling at him. 'How y'all doing? You feel like dining on some sushi? I'm sitting on the garage, I see the maid come out back with a pail of garbage, leftover tuna and avocado rolls she throws in the trash can. Follow me,' Cicero Crow said, 'to the movie-star's house.' He raised his shiny black wings to beat the air, waddled away from them and took off.

'See?' Antwan said. 'Likes doing me favours.'

'He can't get the lid off the garbage can,' Ramona said, 'the only reason he calls you.'

'It works out,' Antwan said. 'See, he thinks he's as smart as us – and crows could be almost as smart. One time I heard Cletus and some old fellas talking about crows, saying if us and them were the only living creatures in the world, which one would get et up. Cletus goes, "If crows are all we have to eat, we'll find a way to catch 'em." Meaning we still smarter but have to look out for 'em. Especially you see a bunch of crows following you.'

He could still scare Ramona when he needed to. Antwan told her to go on home now. 'Me and Cicero do our business one on one.'

Cicero had mentioned the sushi being in a movie-star's trash, but didn't say which movie star. It didn't matter as movie stars always had the best garbage, and the most of it. Like they bought more food than they could eat and had to throw a lot of it away.

Antwan liked Chinese food, came in those white cartons. He liked sushi, fish and rice wrapped up together. He liked pizza with cheese and pepperoni, a nice piece of hamburger with ketchup on it. He even liked broccoli and brussels sprouts. Antwan ran down the hill and through dark woods and came out on an alley that ran behind a huge white house with a wire fence around the backyard. He had looked for food here a number of times before but never knew it belonged to a movie star. Two big trash cans, green ones, stood behind the garage, Cicero perched on one of them.

'Hit it!' Cicero said, and flapped his wings to lift himself up onto the edge of the garage roof, out of the way.

Antwan got ready. Dug his claws into the ground. Lunged in two powerful bounds across the alley. Leaped at the trash can to bounce it off the back of the garage and drop on its side – Cicero *caw-cawing* now, flapping his wings, as Antwan clawed the lid from the big green can and stuck his nose inside.

At this moment the most amazing adventure of his coyote life was about to begin.

two

Antwan came face to face with a mouse trapped inside the trash can, a mouse with wasabi on its little twitching whiskers.

Face to face for only a second and the mouse was gone, out of there with Antwan after it, smelling mouse and sushi, a feast, paying no attention to Cicero cawing at him, 'You crazy? Where you going?'

He chased that mouse to the wire fence that was about five feet high. The mouse scurried right through the wire, and Antwan took a flying leap over the top, came down almost close enough to nip the mouse's tail, looked up and stopped in his tracks.

A dog was in the yard by the swimming pool.

A German shepherd, bigger than Antwan.

There was something familiar about this dog lying in the grass working on a bone. His big white teeth gnawing it clean. The dog raised his head to watch the mouse run past to the house and disappear into a hole. But he didn't bark or chase after it.

Now the dog sat up and looked this way, and Antwan saw the red bandana around his neck: the dog from the park who thought he was stylish and liked to play catch. The dog kept staring at him, so Antwan bushed out his tail and stuck it straight back behind him, ready for business. The dog still didn't bark and get bent out of shape the way most dogs would.

No, this dog was cool for a homeboy, an older male who had peed all over this big yard, marking it to let everybody know this was his turf and nobody else's.

Antwan was thinking, Keep it, homes. Live here and get food handed to you. Believe you're somebody in your pitiful kept world, no better than a slave.

Antwan and the dog kept staring at each other, Antwan wondering what could be on this homey's mind. Now he watched the dog get up and shake the leaves and grass off his butt and walk over to the house. Now he'd stand there helpless and start barking for somebody to let him in.

But he didn't. He walked up to the back door, stood there, and then looked around at Antwan. Like he was saying, Watch. This is how you get in. Next thing, he pushed his head against a dog door that was part of the big door, down low, stepped inside and the flap of the dog door closed behind him.

Weird. Antwan saying to himself, You know what that homey's telling you? He's inviting you in the house.

Yeah, but what if it was a trap and that German dog had a bunch of his brothers in there waiting?

This came to Antwan's mind 'cause he knew you should never trust dogs. Then was gone from his mind 'cause he had no respect for them, either. All they did mostly was bark and fuss, get excited. Dogs gave Antwan a headache.

He wondered should he howl for the Howling Diablos, tell 'em leave whatever you're doing and get over here. Not Antwan or any coyotes he knew of had ever been inside a house. The closest was when they looked in windows to watch TV.

Uh-unh, he couldn't wait – too anxious to see what it was like being inside and not afraid to go in alone. He said to himself, Then do it, man.

With no idea of what he might find going on

in there, Antwan pushed through the door flap and stepped into a house for the first time in his life.

He smelled the dog right away but didn't care or even look to see where he was. Antwan had caught the scent of peanut butter cookies, sitting right on the kitchen table. He hopped up there and ate every last one of the cookies and didn't think of the dog again until he was right there, sitting on the floor, licking his lips as he looked up at Antwan licking his, Antwan thinking there was something wrong with this dog.

He said, 'Homes, can't you smell?'

'Of course I can smell.'

'You know cookies are sitting here and you don't eat none?'

'We're not allowed cookies,' the big German dog said, sounding like a wimp. He turned his head to point to two dog dishes sitting on the floor, each with a name on it. *Buddy* on one, *Miss Betty* on the other.

Antwan said, 'Which one's yours, homes?'

Buddy was giving him a cold look now, serious. He said, 'You don't know who I am, do you?'

'I see you like to wear that hankie around your neck and play catch with your owner. Why should I know who you are?'

Buddy was standing now. All he said was, 'Follow me,' and started out of the kitchen.

'Wait,' Antwan said. 'Who's Miss Betty?'

'She lives here, too. Betty freaked seeing you in the yard. I had to settle her down.'

'She happen to be a show bitch poodle,' Antwan said, 'with a creamy-coloured coat?'

He could tell from the surprised look on Buddy's face he had it right, Miss Betty was the one at the dog park with the two kids.

'Where she at, homes? I like to meet her.'

'You promise not to mess with her?'

'I haven't messed with you, have I?'

'You know better,' Buddy said. 'What do they call you?' Antwan told him and Buddy said, 'Come on, Antwan, but you have to behave yourself.'

Antwan hopped down from the table to follow, walking on his toes the way coyotes do, and the next thing was slipping and sliding on the tile floor. Like a pond frozen over in the winter. They entered the family room and his claws dug into carpeting, soft and deep as grass. He looked around and saw different kinds of chairs, what humans sat on to watch TV, brought his gaze up to the walls and saw a German shepherd in a row of big movie posters, and in every one of them the dog was wearing a red bandana around his neck.

'That's *you*,' Antwan said, amazed. 'I been

15

coming to this house for the fine garbage, it turns out you're the movie star lives here?'

'I made those movies and a few more,' Buddy said, 'till I retired. *Buddy to the Rescue*, *Buddy Goes to War*, *Buddy and the Kidnappers*, *Buddy on Safari* – it was supposed to be in Africa, but they shot all my movies on the backlot of the studio. I played a drug sniffer in *Traffic* but the scene was cut.'

'I think I saw you in one of 'em,' Antwan said, trying not to sound impressed. 'Was either on TV or at the drive-in we go to over by Encino. We sit up on the hill in the summer and watch the movies.'

Buddy said, 'What do you do in the winter?'

'Same as all year, we hunt. There are people that put out food, but not many.'

'And you take it, don't you?'

'It's just sitting there,' Antwan said. He raised his nose and sniffed, catching a scent that seemed part dog and part human, with a soft, powdery smell of flowers thrown in, a scent you'd catch from humans that were female. He started toward the sofa.

Buddy said, 'Betty, he knows you're there. Come on out.'

Antwan stopped in the middle of the room. He watched Miss Betty appear in a timid way, coming out from behind the sofa. Yes indeed, it was the

16

same creamy-coloured poodle from the dog park, all trimmed and tricked out with a blue ribbon and a puff of hair on top of her head, pom-poms around her ankles and one on the tip of her tail. Antwan had to admit, this was the prettiest dog he'd ever seen. He started toward her and Miss Betty backed away, her pom-poms shaking, her big black eyes in that creamy cute face staring at him.

'He knows better than to hurt you,' Buddy said. 'This is Antwan, our first coyote. Let him come over and say hi.'

Betty held still while Antwan approached, came nose to nose with her, the way he had seen humans do it, and said, 'Mmmmm, girl, you smell good enough to eat.'

And Betty was out of that room like the pom-pom on her tail was afire, gone.

Buddy called out to her, 'Betty –' and then turned to Antwan with a mean look. 'What'd you say that for? I had her settled and you scared her to death.'

It surprised Antwan. 'I was being nice.'

'Saying you want to eat her?'

'What I told her was she smelled fine. Same as I tell a sister I think is looking cool.'

Buddy kept staring at him now. The dog didn't get it. Dumb from living with humans. Now he walked over to a front window and stood there looking out for about a minute before he said, 'The family will be home soon, the mom and dad, Cody and little Courtney. Cody plays lacrosse – they're picking him up.'

'What should I do,' Antwan said, 'act dumb and pretend I'm a dog?'

'You leave before they get here. What I do sometimes when I know the dad's coming home – the way you know things?' Buddy said. 'Doesn't matter when. I go sit by the door. The dad walks in, sees me waiting and can't believe it. How could I know he was coming just then?'

'I know humans can't do that,' Antwan said. 'Or tell what another human's thinking. They always asking each other questions. "What'd you do that for?" But still they the ones in charge of things. Tell us where we can live –'

'That's what I don't understand,' Buddy said, 'when we're smarter than they are.'

'What's this *we*?' Antwan said. 'You're more like them than like us. You sold your soul, homes, for some dog food.'

'Twice a day,' Buddy said, 'and a warm, dry place to sleep. Nobody ever shooting at me.'

He had a point there. 'But you're missing the fun of being wild,' Antwan said, 'run around, do anything you want.'

'Would you trade places with me, you had the chance?'

Buddy sounding serious. It surprised Antwan.

He said, 'Would I have to play catch? Sit up and roll over? Be told when I can go outside? Eat pet food?'

Buddy came closer to him saying, 'You think being wild means you can put me down?'

This German dog was half a head taller, way heavier, and had those big teeth.

He said, 'You think I can't run you off, your tail between your skinny legs?'

Antwan stared at the dog thinking of what to do. He said, 'Lemme hear you growl.'

It stopped Buddy. 'You want to know can I growl?'

'I know you *can*, I want to hear you.'

'What kind of growl?'

'A mean one.'

Buddy lowered his head at Antwan and growled, man, like he was ready to tear Antwan apart.

Antwan said, 'Dog, that's a growl. It's the scariest growl I ever heard. But . . . do you think you can make me run if I don't want to? Tail between my skinny legs?'

He paused, ready to answer his own question either way, with a yes or a no, as he looked into Buddy's eyes to judge the dog's temper.

Then didn't have to say anything. They both sensed the car coming at the same time.

'They're here,' Buddy said, sounding both excited and nervous about it. 'It's too late to go out the back. Any second now they'll be pulling up to the garage. You'll have to run upstairs and hide under a bed. I'll come for you later and sneak you out of the house.'

Antwan, showing he was cool, didn't move. He said, 'Dog, I thought you wanted to trade places.' Saying it didn't mean Antwan wanted to. But now he was curious about living in a house instead of a hole in the side of a hill, where if it rained, he'd spend the day in his den nibbling on spiders for something to do.

'I don't want them seeing you for the first time in the house,' Buddy said, still acting twitchy, like he had worms or something. 'It's better they see you outside, get used to your hanging around. You understand? They see us together, see we get along –'

'Like we friends?' Antwan said.

'Like they think you're a cross-breed mutt, part some kind of skinny hound and a few more breeds in your ancestry.'

'Wait now,' Antwan said. 'Hold it right there. You want these humans to believe I'm a *dog*?'

'A coyote is a dog,' Buddy said. 'All you have to do is behave yourself, act like you've had some training.'

'So you can have a coyote around the house? Let your doggy friends think you tamed me?'

'I told you, I'm talking about trading places,' Buddy said. 'You stay here as long as you want. I go up in the hills and join the pack.' He said, 'Antwan,' with a pitiful kind of look on his face, 'I'm tired of being a pet.'

This German dog gave you a lot to think about but no time to do it in. Buddy took Antwan to the front hall where a carpeted staircase curved upstairs, Buddy saying, 'Go on now, quick. Hide under a bed.'

'You have your own room up there?'

'Betty does. I like the kitchen.'

'Close to the food, huh? Get hungry in the night, have yourself a snack.'

'You got to stop thinking about food all the time,' Buddy said. 'When you know you're gonna get fed you don't worry about it.'

'Would I have my own room, like Betty?'

Buddy, acting nervous again, said, 'Will you please get upstairs? I'll come find you.'

'See you when I see you,' Antwan said, and went up the staircase in a few bounds, nothing

YA / 1058278

to it. He roamed along the hall now looking into rooms at the way humans lived, at the big beds they slept on, saw all kind of toys and stuffed animals in two of the rooms – some animals that looked like little bears. But weren't humans afraid of bears? It didn't make sense. Buddy going up to join the pack, thinking he could walk right in and be one of them – that didn't make sense, either. He ever went up there alone they'd jump him before he could say hi. This trading places would never work in a million years.

Antwan smelled water and went into a little room with a slippery floor and a big white bowl had a lid on it against the wall. The water was inside there. Antwan lifted the lid with his nose, then had to lift what looked like a seat, except it had a big hole in it. All this work to stick your face in there and get a drink of water, Antwan thirsty after eating those peanut butter cookies.

There was a big tub in here. Why didn't they fill it with water? Be easier to get a drink, just jump in the tub. Otherwise you'd have to go out to the swimming pool any time you were thirsty. It tasted funny, but it quenched your thirst. Antwan had drunk from many a swimming pool. Every house up in these hills had one.

He sniffed along the hall again. Stopped and felt his ears cock as he heard human voices. Then

hurried to follow the sound, into a room where the window was open.

Antwan looked out to see the backyard and the garage, the mom and dad and the two kids coming toward the house. Cody, the boy, looked a few years older than his little sister, Courtney. Antwan could never tell about kids. Some offered you things to eat and others threw rocks at you.

He watched the family reach the patio that stuck out into the yard, the roof over it just below this window. He could hear them in the house now, the human voices. One of the kids yelling, the boy, Cody. Sounding like a kid who'd throw rocks rather than feed you.

Antwan had raced through this room to the window without noticing what was in here. Now he looked around, catching a familiar scent, and saw the display of trophies and ribbons and pictures in colour of Miss Betty posing and knew he was in her room.

He turned toward the bed, like the ones in the kids' rooms, tiptoed over to it sniffing the air, finding that familiar scent stronger here. Now he stretched out on the floor to check underneath and there she was: Miss Betty's big black eyes looking at him from out of the dark.

Antwan said, 'Hey, girl,' in his nicest tone, 'what're you doing under there?'

three

When Buddy was working in movies, running his tail off doing dangerous stunts all day, he'd come home from the studio worn out, and the kids would be all over him wanting to play. Now that he was retired, hanging around the house all day with Cody and Courtney, they hardly ever wanted to do anything.

When they did, it was to pull tricks on him.

Cody would throw a ball in the swimming pool and say, 'Fetch.' Buddy would jump in, get the ball in his mouth, crawl out of the pool and Cody would be nowhere in sight.

What little Courtney liked to do, she'd say, 'Buddy, stay,' and leave him sitting there all day like a dog made of stone. Except stone dogs didn't have to pee. Buddy would stay as long as he could before racing to the dog door to get outside. He'd hear Courtney yelling, 'Mom, Buddy disobeyed me.'

Cody and Courtney would pretend to wrestle with him and stick bogeys in his hair and roll on the floor laughing. Any time Buddy saw them picking their noses he'd run and hide under a bed. The kids would tell their mom, 'Buddy won't play with us,' in that pouty voice they'd put on, and he'd get yelled at.

Or they'd blame Buddy for something they did all the time. Cody would hold his nose saying, 'Buddy, shame on you.' And Courtney would call to their mom, 'Buddy's letting farts again.'

He couldn't win.

They never played tricks on him when he was making movies. Making a lot of money, too. Enough to buy this big house and fancy cars. He never got yelled at, either.

They were tired of him and now Miss Betty was getting all the attention. A woman came every week in her Pooch Caboose to give Betty a bath and keep her groomed with all those puffs and pom-poms. Betty loved it. She couldn't pass a mirror without stopping to look at herself. She never wanted to play, afraid she might muss up her hair.

This year, Betty was entered in the dog beauty contest and for the first time in her life failed to win Best in Show. Buddy thought, Good. Maybe she won't act so stuck-up now. But the dad and the kids would moan and pet her, telling Betty she really was the best and should've won. What all that did was get Betty feeling sorry for herself. Now she moped around the house or stayed in her room, hardly ever saying a word. It left Buddy more lonely than ever, a pet that never got petted.

What he would do, stretch out on the floor and watch videos of his movies. In every one of them he was able to act out what he wanted to tell people and get them to do something. In *Buddy to the Rescue* he was able to act out the little girl trapped in the cave, wolves closing in on her, and the other actors understood.

But it wasn't the same in real life.

No matter how hard he tried, there was no way to get the family to understand that he was a working dog and needed to keep busy. He'd try acting out how bored he was and the dad would say, 'What's wrong, fella?' He always called him fella. 'You getting lazy, don't want to play with the kids?'

Sometimes in the evening as it was getting dark, Buddy would see coyotes up on the hill, out of their dens for a night of hunting. Getting ready, goofing around with each other. They were dogs, too, but nobody's pets. They were dogs that could do anything they felt like.

Buddy had made up his mind to take off when along came Antwan: somebody to guide him up that hill and introduce him to the pack.

Up in Miss Betty's bedroom Antwan was standing now, looking at the dog show trophies she'd won and the pictures of her posing, Miss Betty still under the bed.

'This all you do?'

She didn't answer.

'Stand around looking pretty?'

Still no answer, too scared to talk.

'You know what?' Antwan said. 'They ought to put coyotes in the dog shows. I don't know any males would do it, but you'd sure see some groovy females.' He waited a moment and said, 'Hey, quit acting like you're scared of me and come on out.'

That did it. Miss Betty slipped out from under the bed and walked by him to the window – Antwan tempted to give the pom-pom on the tip of her tail a friendly nip. She pointed her cute black nose at the window and said, 'This is the way out. Please leave.'

She turned to him now, looked him in the eye, and Antwan saw she wasn't scared of him at all.

Not the least bit. No, she acted the way she did 'cause she was snooty. She was a famous showgirl who won trophies and had no time for coyotes. One thing for sure, though, Miss Betty did not look happy.

'I saw you at the dog park,' Antwan said, 'with the kids. You didn't look like you were having much fun. Don't you ever get out by yourself and run around in the woods, see what you can scare up?'

All Miss Betty said to that was, 'You have to go.'

'I know,' Antwan said. 'Hey, but I could come back sometime, take you for a run in the woods.' Antwan thinking it would be cool if she said yeah, why don't you?

She didn't though. Miss Betty cocked her head like she was listening to something and said, 'Courtney's looking for me.'

Downstairs in the kitchen, Courtney was saying to her mom sipping a cold beverage as the dad made himself one, 'I can't find her anywhere.'

Cody said, 'You haven't even looked.'

'I have so.'

'You have not.'

'Have so.'

The mom pushed her hair away from her face and said, 'Cody, knock it off.'

The dad said, 'Hey, fella,' and Buddy looked up. The dad said something about Betty, Buddy catching the name. He knew enough human words to figure out they were looking for her. Yeah, the dad pointing to the dog door. Calling him fella again, telling him to go look outside.

The way it was in this life – Antwan was right – all he did was what *they* wanted. But Betty was probably upstairs, and so was Antwan . . . There was no way to warn him, so Buddy did what he was told. He went outside.

The mom said to Courtney, 'I'll bet she's up in her room. Have you looked there?'

Antwan was beginning to feel sorry for Miss Betty. She didn't choose to be a showgirl. It was what *they* wanted her to be. Betty did what she was told and now was stuck with a life of posing and looking pretty. Antwan wondered if he could help her.

He said, 'I bet you never got burrs in your pom-poms.'

She said, 'Will you please leave?'

He tried a different approach. 'You know what me and Buddy been talking about?'

She said, 'Me, I suppose.'

'That's one of your problems,' Antwan said, 'always thinking about yourself.' He could tell she didn't like that, so he said right away, 'Buddy wants us to trade places.'

She looked surprised and then interested. 'How could you do that?'

'He joins the coyotes and I stay here, pretend I'm a dog.'

Was that a smile on her cute face? It looked like one. Now she was shaking her head.

'It would never work. You don't have manners or know how to act like a dog.'

It encouraged Antwan she was willing to talk about it. He said, 'Buddy thinks we can pull off the switch. And if I was here, girl, I could show you how to run around and have some fun. Show you sights you wouldn't believe till you saw 'em. There's a whole world out there you're missing.'

Miss Betty hesitated now, looking into his eyes like she wanted to hear more or catch a glimpse of this world he was talking about. Her gaze moved past him then, her expression changing to a look of surprise, and she said, 'Oh, no . . .'

Antwan turned his head to see Courtney standing in the doorway. Courtney there and then gone, running down the hall and yelling as loud as she could:

'A coyote's in the house!'

*

Betty was by the open window now, motioning for Antwan to go out, telling him, 'Quick, jump!' She watched him leap through the opening to land on the roof over the patio, watched him slide down the shingles, jump to the ground and run for the fence.

Now she saw Buddy in the yard, Buddy coming around the swimming pool to run after Antwan like he was chasing him.

But he wasn't.

She couldn't believe her eyes as she saw Antwan and Buddy go over the fence together side by side. Gone.

The family came from the hall into Betty's room, all of them with something to say. First the dad pretended to look around the room. He said to Courtney, 'Sweetheart, I don't see a coyote,' sounding like he was serious.

Cody said, 'You don't believe her, do you? A coyote just happens to be in the house?'

'It was,' Courtney said, 'it was right here in this room.'

'She makes up stories to get attention.'

'Cody,' the mom said, 'stay out of it.'

'She does it all the time. And then cries.'

Tears showed in Courtney's eyes.

'See?' Cody said.

'I *saw* it,' Courtney said, sobbing now. 'Betty knows I'm telling the truth.'

Miss Betty looked up hearing her name and wagged her stylish tail. She said, 'Courtney's right, a coyote was in my room,' but all the family heard were a few yips and a growl.

The dad walked over to the window saying, 'Buddy was in the backyard.' He looked out. 'But I don't see him now.' He put two fingers to his mouth, and the blast of his whistle filled the room.

The mom closed her eyes. She opened them and said, 'Why don't we go downstairs and have a cold drink?'

Betty waited for them to leave before going to the window. She looked out at the hillside, her eyes on the open slope above the trees, but saw no sign of Antwan or Buddy. She began wondering what it would be like to be with them.

To miss her grooming appointments and run free.

Antwan loped all the way through the woods to the bare part of the hill before he stopped and waited for Buddy to catch up.

'I thought I'd lose you,' Antwan said, as Buddy reached him and sat down. 'You're pretty fast for an old-timer.'

'I'm not too old,' Buddy said, 'to sniff your trail and hunt you down. I'm ready to see where you live and meet the family.'

'Homes, you might think you're ready,' Antwan said. 'If you were a wild dog, it would be different. Wild dogs can catch on to our ways. But you're nothing but a house pet, used to your little doggy dish, your name on it.'

'I know who I am and what I can do,' Buddy said. 'What I'm tired of is being told what to do. I want to see what it's like to live in the wild. Stay out all night and chase after game.'

'Like squirrels and rabbits?' Antwan said.

'I love chasing squirrels and rabbits.'

'How about cats?'

'I've chased hundreds of cats.'

'But did you eat 'em?'

'Look,' Buddy said, standing up now, bigger than this skinny coyote with the pointy ears, Buddy convinced he was every bit as brave, 'I can chase what I want and eat what I want, in a dish or on the ground. I'm not taking any more of your smart-alec insults. You say one more word about me being a pet, I'll bite your bushy tail off and make you eat it.'

It got Antwan thinking, maybe this dog did have the chops to make the switch work. The pack would give Buddy a hard time, see how tough he was, but he'd stand up to 'em and give it back, wouldn't he? The pack would have to agree, Buddy was cool, for a dog.

No, the problem was Antwan pulling off his part in the scheme. He said to Buddy, 'You want me to introduce you to my family.'

'That's all,' Buddy said, 'then it's up to me.'

'But what am I supposed to do, just walk in the house and say hi y'all? I need you there, homes, to show 'em we friends. I can't hope for Miss Betty to help me. That girl hardly ever speaks.'

Buddy saw what he meant and began nodding his head.

'You're right, we don't want to jump the gun. We better do the hard part first, get you settled in the house before we go up the hill.' Buddy paused then, narrowing his eyes at Antwan. 'If you think this is a joke and you're playing some kind of trick on me –'

Antwan shook his head and looked Buddy in the eye to show he was serious. He said, 'Homes, the only tricky part is getting your people to believe I'm a dog. Getting *me* to believe it, too, so I can try to act like one.' He said, 'Listen, you go on home and I'll see you tonight. Wait for me in the kitchen. Then in the morning, introduce me as your new friend.'

Buddy was thinking about something now,

34

nodding his head again. He said, 'You need a dog collar.'

'Man, we got all kinds of 'em.'

'Bring one.'

Now Antwan was nodding. 'That's an idea. Yeah, but how do I get it on?'

'I'll think of a way,' Buddy said.

Ramona wanted to join the Howling Diablos, but Antwan wouldn't let her, even though two girls were in the gang. Antwan said, 'When you can hunt with Iris and Grace you're in the posse. You have to know things. You hear a rabbit crying – is the bunny in trouble, or is it a human blowing his lure? They sound the same. You come running and he shoots you. Whenever you run you're looking everywhere, and when you're out in the open, you watch the sky.'

These words were in Ramona's mind almost in the same moment she heard the crow – too late to watch the sky and now she was afraid to look up, see a ring of crows circling to dive at her. She kept running, faster now, then stopped in her tracks as Cicero Crow landed on a rock, about three leaps in front of her.

'You didn't hear me calling? I bet you didn't hear about Antwan, either. About him going in the house with the police dog? Not like Antwan was busted, or like he was gonna eat the dog. Just went in the house. But listen, I got one for him, a cute white Persian they let out in the yard, the new kitty in the neighbourhood. Her name's Lola.'

Ramona said, 'He went in a house?'

'And came out. Listen, tell Antwan to give me a howl.'

She climbed to the pack's grounds and found Antwan coming out of a slit in the rock wall, his den.

She said, 'You were in a house,' sounding amazed.

Antwan said, 'I know I was. What I like you to do, find me a dog collar, one that will go around my poor neck.'

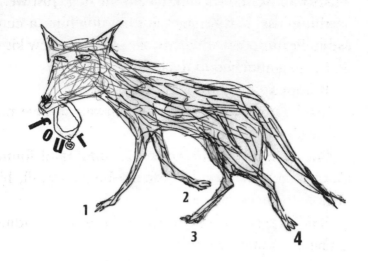

Antwan arrived not long past midnight, the house dark except for a light showing in the kitchen.

Buddy, waiting for him in the yard, watched Antwan jump the fence and come across the lawn, a dog collar hanging from his mouth. 'Let's go inside,' Buddy said. He led the way through the dog door and into the kitchen. Antwan dropped the collar on the floor.

'They all sleeping?'

'The kids. The mom and dad fall asleep watching TV. Tonight it's *Saturday Night Live*. You want something to eat?'

'You mean *food* or dog food?'

'There's some kibbles in Betty's dish she hardly touched.'

Antwan went over and stuck his nose in the dish, catching Miss Betty's scent but not much taste to it as he began to eat. Buddy now was looking at the licence tag attached to the collar lying on the floor.

'It says your name's Timmy, but I can't read the rest. This tag looks like somebody was chewing on it.'

Antwan raised his head from the kibbles. 'I did that, homes, so they'll know my name but won't be able to check me out.'

'You're pretty smart,' Buddy said.

'You just finding that out?'

'What happened to this dog Timmy?'

'I wouldn't be surprised some coyotes had him for supper,' Antwan said, 'before my time. I don't recognize the collar.' He ate some more kibbles before looking up again. 'Was this Timmy a friend of yours?'

'I knew a little schnauzer answers to that name,' Buddy said, 'a show dog, but that collar would've been too big for him.'

'I tried sticking my head through it,' Antwan said, finished with the kibbles, 'but couldn't work it past my ears. How'm I gonna get it on?'

'What I have in mind,' Buddy said, 'I see little Courtney helping you.'

'How you get her to do that?'

'Act it out,' Buddy said. 'Don't worry, I'll tell

you what to do when the time comes. The collar's gonna be part of the show, getting them to believe you're some strange kind of dog.'

'We do it here in the kitchen?'

'Outside,' Buddy said, 'while they're having their Sunday breakfast on the patio. I see by the sky it's gonna be nice tomorrow. So the kids will be in the pool or playing around it. I'm talking about when we make our move.'

'You sure it's gonna work?'

'Trust me,' Buddy said. 'We go out at sunrise and hide in the shrubs back of the swimming pool. We wait till the mom and dad are having their breakfast before we come out and walk toward the house. You keep your head and your tail down and only do what I tell you.'

Antwan said, 'You let Miss Betty know about it?'

'She'll be watching from upstairs,' Buddy said, 'I'm pretty sure. This'll be good for her. Give her something to think about besides herself.'

The next morning, Antwan and Buddy came out of the shrubs and started across the lawn, Antwan with the collar hanging from his jaws.

Courtney, in her swimsuit, was running from the house to the pool. She didn't see them right away.

Cody did, standing on the diving board, but only stared, too surprised to say anything.

Now Courtney saw them and called out, 'Dad . . . ?' not sure whether or not to be afraid.

The mom and dad were having breakfast on the patio, each reading a section of the Sunday paper. The dad, intent on entertainment news, didn't look up when Courtney called the first time, or when she called again, 'Da-ad!' louder.

The mom, with a glass of what appeared to be tomato juice, didn't look up, either, since she wasn't the dad.

'Be cool,' Buddy said to Antwan. 'Put your tail down.'

'I can't help it,' Antwan said. 'I get excited it sticks out by itself.' He looked up at Miss Betty's window and there she was, watching. He thought of giving her a howl, but Buddy had told him, 'No howling. The last thing you want to do is howl and give yourself away.'

Courtney yelled again, 'Da-ad!'

The mom looked up from the Book Review section. 'Courtney wants you.'

The dad, behind his newspaper, said, 'What?' and kept reading. The mom, her back to the yard, sipped her juice.

'Stay here,' Buddy said to Antwan, 'while I go see Courtney. I look around, you come with your

40

head low, like you're telling them they're the boss, you're just a dog.'

Cody kept staring at Antwan, squinting his eyes. He said to Courtney, 'You ever see that dog before?'

'It's not a dog,' Courtney said, 'it's a coyote,' but didn't know what to do about it. Now Buddy came over to her and began touching her with his nose and licking her hand.

Now he looked up at her little girl face with soul in his eyes. As soon as she started petting him he motioned for Antwan to get over here. He came with the dog collar and Buddy said, 'Drop it in front of her. Okay, now you think you can take Courtney's hand in your mouth and put it on the collar?'

'In my mouth?'

'Without chewing on it?'

Antwan said, 'Man, I don't know.'

'Forget it,' Buddy said. 'What we have to do is show the child you're a nice doggy.' He began nuzzling Antwan – Antwan making a face – and licking him, and now Buddy was making a face. Pretty soon Courtney was reaching out to Antwan.

Her hand touched his shoulder, Antwan's tail shot out, and Buddy said, 'Listen to me, wild man,' growling the words, 'you're a little doggy that wants to be petted. When you look up at her, soften your eyes.' Watching him Buddy said, 'Yeah, that's good. Now wag your tail.'

Antwan said, 'Should I lick her?'

'Let her make the first move.'

'I never licked a human before.'

Cody stood with his toes curled over the edge of the diving board. He said, 'That's no coyote.'

'It is too,' Courtney said.

'If it was a real one he'd be eating you by now.'

Antwan said to Buddy, 'Now should I lick her?'

'Yeah, then pick up the collar and give it to her.'

'What if she won't take it?'

'She will, she saw the movie where I do it. Courtney likes to be handed things.'

'I could get the child a rabbit, even one's not dead.'

Antwan handed Courtney the collar. She took it and sat down in the grass and then spent some time to buckle it, Buddy saying, 'The little girl in the movie was a whole lot quicker.'

Cody, still on the diving board, turned to the patio and yelled, 'Dad! Look at Courtney!'

The note of urgency in Cody's voice got the dad to knock over his coffee as he brought the news-paper down, quick, and looked out at the yard. He saw his two children and his two . . . No, there were two dogs, but one of them wasn't his.

'Cody, where'd he come from?'

'I don't know. Buddy brought him.'

'It's the coyote,' Courtney said, 'that was in the house.'

Cody said, 'She thinks it's a coyote.'

The mom turned her chair sideways to have a look as the dad stepped out to the edge of the patio. He said, 'What's Courtney doing?'

'Fixing his collar.'

'A dog collar?'

'It must've come off,' Cody said.

The mom sipped her juice and said, 'Why don't you see if there's a licence?'

The dad started across the lawn waving his arm at Courtney. 'Step away from him, sweetheart. There's no telling where he's been. He could have rabies.'

Buddy said to Antwan, 'Walk toward the dad wagging your tail. When he says "Stay," stop and raise your head. He wants to look at the tag on the collar. Then you come back this way and I bct he calls you by name.'

Antwan said, like he was serious, 'He's gonna call me Antwan?'

Buddy didn't think it was funny. He said, 'You want this to work or not?'

The mom got up and came out on the lawn with her juice. She said to the dad, 'I think they're

43

talking to each other.' The dad didn't seem to hear her. 'They give each other little woofs and snarls,' the mom said, 'and nod their heads.'

Antwan turned from Courtney and walked toward the dad until the dad said, 'Stay,' and Antwan stopped in his tracks. Then added something of his own to the act. He raised one paw, stuck his tail out and leaned forward pointing his nose, the way he'd seen hunting dogs do it at the park.

The dad looked back at the mom, then hunched down to find the tag on the collar, ready to jump away if he heard a growl. He rose saying, 'There's no licence, and the I.D. looks like it's been chewed. I can't read the address, only his name.'

'Well, what is it?' the mom said.

The dad held a hand up for her to be quiet. He waited as Antwan walked away, got almost as far as Buddy and Courtney before he said, 'Timmy?'

Antwan stopped and looked around.

'Sit,' the dad said.

Antwan didn't move, not till he heard Buddy, behind him, woof, 'Sit down.'

Antwan sat. And the dad announced to the family, 'Timmy's a dog.'

What they did now was try to decide what kind of dog Timmy was.

'What's the big deal,' Cody said, 'he's a skinny German shepherd.'

The mom said, 'I think Cody's right.'

'He definitely has some shepherd in him,' the dad said. 'I would guess there's also a spaniel in his lineage, a pointer, possibly a setter.' He said in a thoughtful kind of way, 'You know what? Maybe even some basenji.'

The mom said, 'You know what a basenji looks like?'

'I know they never bark,' the dad said. 'Have you heard Timmy bark? I haven't.'

Buddy, lying in the grass with Antwan, said, 'They're talking about you. You hear them say, "Timmy," cock your pointy ears and look up.'

Cody said, 'I think he's a junkyard dog.'

'Whatever he is,' the mom said, 'what do we do with him?'

Courtney said, 'I don't care what he is,' and came over and got down next to Antwan and put her arms around his neck, tight, like she would never let go.

Antwan squirmed and Buddy said to him, 'Easy, boy.'

'What's she doing?'

'Letting the mom and dad know she loves you,' Buddy said. 'Telling them if you don't get to stay here it will break her heart. She'll cry and carry on, won't eat, won't do what she's told, until the mom and dad say to her, "All right, but he's your dog, you'll have to take care of him."'

Antwan said, 'Her hugging me says all that?'

'It means you have a home,' Buddy said. He paused now to look at the family on the patio having their breakfast and then at Antwan again.

Something on his mind. Antwan could tell.

'What's wrong?'

Buddy said, 'You know what it means they say a dog is housebroken?'

Antwan said, 'No, what?'

Buddy said, 'Uh-oh.'

All day long Buddy kept asking Antwan if he had to pee, and Antwan would say, 'No – quit bothering me.'

'When you do, be sure you go in the backyard.'

'But that's your ground out there, you marked it.'

'You can mark over my mark, it's okay. Just don't go in the house.'

'Why would I? I don't go in my den.'

After that Buddy quit asking him.

Antwan complained about the dry dog food. 'There's no taste to it.'

'It's good for you,' Miss Betty said, like that would make it taste better.

'Why don't they let us eat the garbage?' Antwan

said. 'Then the maid won't have to take it outside.'

Miss Betty said, 'Yuck,' making a face, like eating garbage was the worst thing she ever heard of.

Antwan said, 'Don't knock it if you haven't tried it. You too used to food comes out of a bag. That's what I'd call being housebroken, not the other thing, peeing on the carpet. You been in the house so long you've lost your taste for regular food.'

What Antwan had the most trouble with was knocking over things. Bump a table and the vase sitting there would fall on the floor and break. Hear a sudden noise, a radio turned on, his tail shot out, hit a bowl of flowers and got water all over the carpet. Anything he did like that, Buddy would give him a lecture on being careful.

It didn't make sense to Antwan. What you had to be careful of were live things, not vases and bowls. See you don't step on snakes or get skunks looking ugly at you.

He had trouble catching on to human speech, what the words meant when he was told not to do something. It would surprise him that they'd act mad and he'd think, What – what'd I do? 'You keep hearing them talk,' Miss Betty said, 'you'll start to pick it up. Listen to the tone of voice and how they move their bodies. But don't let on you know everything they're saying.'

'Just obey the easy commands,' Buddy said, 'and that'll make them happy.'

'I haven't been told yet to roll over,' Antwan said and looked at Miss Betty. 'I'll roll over for you if you'll check me for fleas.'

Trying to be funny – but dogs didn't always understand coyote humour.

Miss Betty said, 'I have a lady who grooms me,' still snooty but starting to come around, interested in helping him become a dog.

'I get good at obeying,' Antwan said, 'I'll enter the dog show with you, the beauty contest.'

Miss Betty stuck her black nose in the air saying, 'You have to be purebred.'

'I'm pure lean and mean coyote,' Antwan said. 'When you're ready for a run in the woods, lemme know.'

She never said she would, but Antwan was pretty sure now she was thinking about it.

The kids played with him the first few days. Courtney would hug him and the next thing they'd be wrestling in the grass, the child not realizing Antwan could clamp his jaws around her throat and drag her into the shrubs. Antwan had to keep telling himself to act like her little doggy.

Buddy said, 'They'll get tired of you and start playing tricks,' and told Antwan what to look out for.

So one time when he was in the kitchen with Courtney and she said, 'Stay,' and walked away, Antwan did too as soon as she was gone. He watched out for her then, made sure he knew where she was. He went outside twice that morning to leave his mark. And when he saw her heading for the kitchen, Antwan got there first and put himself in his 'Stay' position. Courtney came in and yelled to her mom, 'Mom, Timmy never goes to the bathroom!'

Outside with Cody – this happened a couple of times – Cody throws the ball in the pool and says, 'Fetch.'

Antwan doesn't move. He says, 'I got your "fetch". You want the ball, kid, go get it yourself.'

And Cody yells to his mom, 'Mom, Timmy's growling at me!'

The mom said, 'Growl back at him.'

One time Cody pushed him in the swimming pool while he was getting a drink of water, Buddy sitting there watching. He said to Antwan later, 'You don't drink out of the pool, it's full of chemicals.'

'It's easier than lifting the lid on that bowl,' Antwan said, 'and then raising the seat with the big hole in it.'

'You dummy,' Buddy said, 'that's where humans

go to the bathroom. You don't drink out of that, either.' He showed Antwan a dish in the kitchen the maid always kept full of water, and said, 'That's your water.'

Buddy was helpful, but less friendly and patient as the days went by, starting to call Antwan a dummy and a numbskull when he was slow catching on to a dog's way of living – most of the things not making sense to him. Antwan was getting all the attention now – from the kids, from Miss Betty, even the maid – and he wondered if maybe Buddy was jealous. The former movie star was spending more time by himself, lying on the floor in the family room watching *Buddy to the Rescue* and the other ones over and over.

Antwan liked the maid. She spoke a different way than the family, using words he and the Howling Diablos would sometimes hear when they went down to the streets at night and checked out the trash behind grocery stores and restaurants. Antwan would see the maid wrapping table scraps to take out. He'd lick his lips and give her that soft look he'd learned if you wanted to be petted or get a treat, and she'd put the scraps in his dish that had *Timmy* on it. She looked at him and said things like she knew it wasn't his name. Antwan offered his table scraps to Buddy one time and Buddy said, 'I don't eat garbage.'

'Then you'll never make it as a coyote,' Antwan said. 'We love garbage, movie stars' the best.'

He told Miss Betty about the change in Buddy, how he was keeping to himself and watching his old movies. Miss Betty said, 'I know,' and Antwan could tell she felt sorry for the old German dog. 'As they say in showbiz, he's over the hill,' Miss Betty said. 'His name doesn't sell tickets any more.'

'Like coyotes that get too old to hunt,' Antwan said, 'and just lie around.'

'If he could act in movies again,' Miss Betty said, 'he'd be a happy dog. You *know*, he only wants to be a coyote because he's bored. And he's bored because he's not acting.'

Wait now – that didn't make sense to Antwan.

'You think pretending to be somebody else is better than being who you are?'

'What you *do* becomes your life,' Miss Betty said, 'and that's who you are.' He caught a glimpse of her snooty look again, like she knew everything, the showgirl saying now, 'That's what you're doing, isn't it?'

'Only to help Buddy get out of the house,' Antwan said. 'There's no way I want to become a dog, live trapped like this? I'd bite off a paw to get out.'

'You could've fooled me,' Miss Betty said.

*

The day the groomer arrived in her Pooch Caboose and parked in the driveway, there was even more of a change in Betty.

Buddy went in first. He came out in thirty minutes looking the same. Betty went in. She came out in an hour looking pretty much the same, but smelling like the mom when the mom got dressed up to go out. It hid her real smell.

'Ready?' Buddy said to Antwan. 'It's your turn.'

No, he wasn't ready. He'd never had a bath in his life, or even knew what a bath was. He went in the Pooch Caboose a coyote and came out forty minutes later feeling like, not quite a bitch, but a girlish dog.

'It's amazing,' Betty said, with a look on her face Antwan had never seen before. 'You look different, not quite, you know, so wild. Mmmmm and you smell' – she began to grin – 'good enough to eat.'

It got Antwan thinking that the Pooch Caboose wasn't a bad deal. He thought the groomer in there was going to drown him, but her hands felt good rubbing him, and he got used to the scissors sniffing at him from nose to tail.

He said, 'You don't think I look funny?'

'Check it out,' Miss Betty said, now and then sounding like him.

They went inside the house to a full-length mirror and Antwan looked at himself, Miss Betty watching. He saw a coyote in the mirror that looked close enough to be taken for any coyote he'd ever seen.

He said to her, 'What looks different about me?'

She said, 'You were shampooed, combed out, trimmed, scented, your Timmy collar shined –'

'It didn't turn me into a dog.'

'I said you don't look as wild, that's all.'

'But what's different?'

'I just told you.'

'I can see I'm still a coyote. How have I changed?'

'Maybe it's just something I feel,' Miss Betty said, 'that we've become more alike.'

'Uh-unh,' Antwan said, 'we can't be more different. Girl, you're tame and I'm wild, I run in the woods.'

She said, 'Have you ever thought of eating me?'

He said, 'No. Well, maybe for one second.'

'You said you wanted to.'

'I know, but I was just being friendly. I'd never been close to a showgirl before.'

'Let me tell you something,' Miss Betty said. 'Before any of us were *show*girls – as you call us, thinking you're cool – and you look back at our ancestry –'

'I bet way back.'

'What I'm trying to say is, my breed started out born retrievers. It's in our blood.'

'Dressed like that, with the pom-poms?'

He couldn't get her to smile.

She said, 'I'm doing something else now, shows, and it's an honour to be chosen.'

'It's your life,' Antwan said, 'so it's who you are. You told me that yourself.'

She said, 'All right, you want to run in the woods? Let's go run in the woods.'

'You mean it?'

'Yes, let's go.'

'You'll feel your heart beating,' Antwan said.

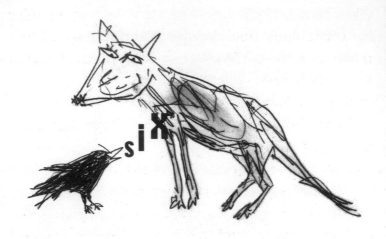

six

From a spot low on the hill Ramona could look down a ravine and see the house and most of the backyard. She had come here every day to watch for Antwan, hoping to see him jump the fence and run up the hill toward her. She was beginning to worry he was never coming home.

Yesterday Cicero Crow had stopped by to ask about Antwan. Ramona told him her brother was still in the house.

'Don't they know he's a coyote?'

'It's weird,' Ramona said. 'I see him playing with the dogs, with the kids. One of 'em even pushed him in the swimming pool.'

'What'd he do to the kid?'

'Nothing. That's what's so weird.'

'So you haven't mentioned the cat to him,' Cicero said, 'Lola, the one they let out in the backyard alone. She's Persian, I'm pretty sure. She might even be a show cat, 'cause whatever Lola wants, Lola gets.'

'What colour is she?'

'What difference does it make? They all taste the same.'

'Antwan likes black cats the best.'

' 'Cause he's reckless, likes to push his luck,' Cicero said. 'This one's pure white with a little pink nose and those tiny ears they have. Walks around the yard looking like cotton candy with legs. I'll see you, little mama,' Cicero said and flew off.

Ramona stretched out again in the brush, holding her long-range coyote gaze on the house. She was learning to be patient and not move, let the rabbit or mouse nibble its way closer – and then pounce before it caught your scent and freaked.

She watched the mom and dad come out of the house with the kids and go to the garage. Ramona sat up. She watched the family drive off in their car. Just the family. The maid had left before. That meant Antwan was alone in the house with the big German dog and the stuck-up poodle. Ramona couldn't stand to watch her walk: like she was saying, Hey, everybody, look at me.

Ramona was thinking now, What if they gang

up on him? And no Diablos around when he needed them. She knew what she'd do if she was a Howling Diablo, she'd howl and get down there quick to help Antwan fight off the homies.

She was so sure her brother was in danger, Ramona howled and raced down the ravine, reached the alley and went over the fence, streaked for the house and then stopped in the yard as she saw the dog door swing open.

First Antwan appeared.

Now the show poodle came, doing her strut.

'Ramona,' Antwan said, being cool, 'this is Miss Betty. Miss Betty, this is my little sister, Ramona. We were just going for a run in the woods. You like to come?'

That was what they did, the three of them, ran across the side of the hill through the trees and brush, sniffing, Antwan showing Miss Betty good places to sniff. Ramona wondering what was going on here. Miss Betty got to chase a rabbit, ran a long way after it zigging and zagging and came back empty, her tongue hanging out. Ramona heard her say to Antwan, 'You're right, you feel your heart beating.'

It told Ramona the two had spent time together talking about serious things.

They came to Cicero Crow sitting on the low

branch of a tree. Antwan saw him first. He told them to wait here while he talked to the crow.

Ramona said to Miss Betty, both of them watching Antwan, 'The crow's telling him about this beautiful cat they let loose in the yard by herself, a white Persian with a pink nose, trying to get by on her looks. You ever hear of such a thing?'

She waited for this Miss Betty to say something, Ramona still not looking at her. When she didn't answer, Ramona said, 'Antwan will snatch that cat before she can meow and have her for supper.' Then gave Miss Betty a sly look. 'You like cats?'

'I can't say I've ever had any as close friends,' Miss Betty said.

'I mean to eat,' Ramona said, but now didn't get an answer. Cicero was flying off, Antwan watching the direction he took before coming over to them.

'He says there's a cat I ought to see. Goes by the name of Lola and lives over that way.'

Miss Betty said, 'We have to be home before the family gets back.'

Ramona didn't like the way she said it, like it was Antwan's home, too. Antwan said, 'I'd just like to have a look at this cat Cicero's so proud of finding.'

Miss Betty surprised Ramona then, the showy

poodle saying, 'What if you took the cat, but not to eat it?'

It seemed Miss Betty had an idea, but wouldn't tell what it was until she thought about it some more.

They came to the house where the cat lived and looked down at it from the side of the hill. It was in a canyon, a huge house that seemed part of the land, kind of a pinkish colour, with different levels and wings and terraces sticking out, a sandcastle that looked like it had grown there.

'Uh-oh,' Ramona said, looking at the fence that enclosed the backyard: a chain-link fence at least ten feet high, topped with a coil of razor wire.

Lola, her fluffy coat silvery in the sunlight, was lying in the grass, playing with – it looked like a rubber mouse, a red one.

Ramona said, 'That cat has to be worth a lot.'

Miss Betty said, 'I was hoping the same thing.'

Antwan said, 'I like black ones, but she'll do.'

Miss Betty frowned. 'Would you really eat her?'

'Whatever he leaves,' Ramona said, 'I'll finish.'

Antwan turned to Miss Betty. 'What do you have in mind?'

'It doesn't matter,' she said, looking at the fence around the yard. 'Lola's safe, since you can't get to her.'

'You want to bet?' Antwan said.

Miss Betty was looking at him again in a way that bothered Ramona, this showy poodle acting like she knew everything, saying now, 'You think you could grab Lola without anyone seeing you?'

'I do it all the time,' Antwan said.

'And promise you won't eat her?'

Was she out of her mind? Ramona wondered if carrying all that fancy hair made it hard for Miss Poodle to think. She heard her brother ask, 'Why would I promise you that?' Being nice. Instead of telling her to get lost.

'Bring the cat here,' Miss Betty said – sounding to Ramona like a smarty, so sure of herself – 'and if you don't agree with what I have in mind for Lola, I'll even help you eat her.'

Some deal. But Antwan seemed to like it. He said, 'Be right back.'

They watched him take off through the trees and didn't see him again until he was down by the fence looking at Lola. Now they watched the cat with nothing to worry about walk over to Antwan and begin talking to him.

'She's telling him to forget it,' Ramona said. 'Saying to Antwan, "You ain't getting over this fence, so don't even think about it." Am I right?'

'Something like that, I suppose,' Miss Betty said.

'See, I thought you and Lola were enough alike,'

Ramona said, 'you'd know what she's saying. You both being in shows and all.'

'Don't hate me because I'm beautiful,' Miss Betty said. 'I can't help it.'

It surprised Ramona, the truth of Miss Betty's words leaving her a bit stunned, and she didn't know what to say.

Miss Betty was looking toward the yard again. She said, 'Where's Antwan?' sounding worried about him.

Ramona changed her voice to a friendlier tone saying, 'He went around to the other side of the house. You'll see him in a minute.' As they waited, watching the house, Ramona said, 'You know I was kidding about you and the cat being alike.'

'I know,' Miss Betty said.

'I was being funny.'

Miss Betty said, 'I'm not trying to change your brother, so don't worry about it. If Antwan doesn't want to learn manners, so be it. Understand what I'm saying to you?'

Sounding like him a little. Maybe he was changing *her*.

Ramona let it go, because now she saw Antwan and said, 'There he is, on the house. He must've jumped onto a low place on the other side.'

Now they caught glimpses of him moving from one level to another, leaping to a deck, running down steps to the terrace, over the railing and he was in the yard.

Lola was taking it easy, playing with the rubber mouse again. 'You can tell she don't know about Antwan,' Ramona said. 'Watch how quick he is. Lola smells him, looks up. Too late, he's got hold of her collar in his teeth. Now Lola's screaming for her kitty life as Antwan runs with her, that cat on a ride she won't ever forget. Look at him, on the terrace now and up the steps, leaps to that deck – look at him – goes up and over the roof with the cat. And there's the human coming out . . . Now she's looking around. She heard Lola scream, but where was she? Calling to her now, "Lola, where are you, honey?" Can't believe the cat's gone. She runs in the house . . . Now she's screaming at somebody maybe was supposed to be watching Lola. You can tell that woman don't know nothing about coyotes. Must've moved here from some-place they don't have any. Except our pack leader, Cletus, says we're everywhere 'cause we know how to stay alive. He says coyotes and crows could be the last ones left on earth on account of our smart brains. Hey, here comes Antwan, like he's carrying a sack of cat hair.'

Antwan brought Lola over to them, unclenched his teeth and shook his head. Lola dropped to the ground stiff-legged, her back humped. Antwan

63

nosed at her and took the paw she threw at him in his mouth. He licked it, let go of it and said to Lola, 'Now settle down. We have to decide if you get et or not.' He looked at Miss Betty. 'Now what?'

'You weren't seen, were you?'

'No, he wasn't seen.' Ramona scowling. 'You could see how that human was looking every which way but up at the house.'

Lola looking from one to the other with big eyes.

'So she won't believe a coyote could have snatched her cat.'

'She won't even think of it,' Ramona said. 'Nobody will.'

'Would Lola leave home by herself? Run away?'

'If she's stupid.'

Lola meowed a pitiful sound.

Antwan listened, waiting for the right question. He already had an idea where this was going.

Miss Betty said, 'So what will they think happened to Lola?'

There it was.

'She was kidnapped by bad guys,' Antwan said, and saw Miss Betty smile.

She said, 'You saw the movie.'

Antwan nodded. '*Buddy and the Kidnappers.*' He had seen the picture with Buddy lying on the floor in the family room. 'Buddy rescues a famous dog

64

entertainer from the kidnappers,' Antwan said, 'a little chihuahua named Pedro.'

'Yes, and Buddy carries him by the collar during the escape,' Miss Betty said, 'the same way you brought Lola here.'

'Who does Buddy rescue her from?'

'Us. We keep her a few days and then Buddy takes her back home.'

'We pass up a good nourishing meal,' Antwan said, 'just to cheer Buddy up?'

'It's been a long time,' Miss Betty said, 'since Buddy's acted like himself. Yes, I want to cheer him up. Buddy's a good old guy. I want to make him a hero again.'

'Wait a minute,' Ramona said, looking up from sniffing Lola, Lola cringing. 'Where you gonna hide her? We take her up to the dens, she'd be et in two minutes.'

Antwan, grinning, said, 'Can you imagine explaining it to Cletus? "No, sir, you can't eat her. We have to keep her for this kidnapping thing we're putting on."' Antwan said to Miss Betty then, 'You gonna hide her in the house?'

'In my closet. I'm sure I can keep her quiet.'

'Show her your trophies,' Antwan said and paused for a moment. 'Will Buddy know she's there?'

'That's a good question,' Miss Betty said. 'Once

we show him Lola and tell him the plan, he might not go for it.'

'Why not?'

'Buddy has his pride. And he's not a hero if it's a hoax.'

Antwan said, 'That's all actors do.'

'This is different,' Miss Betty said. 'We have to decide, do we tell him or not?'

By the time Antwan and Miss Betty had sent Ramona home and gotten back to the house with Lola – only minutes before the family car pulled into the garage – they had decided not to tell Buddy their scheme to make him a hero.

'I'm afraid,' Miss Betty said, 'he'll refuse to have anything to do with it. But then you'll want to have Lola for supper and I can't bear to see that happen.'

'Then don't look,' Antwan said.

Wrong. He should've learned by now Miss Betty didn't think he was funny.

'We have to work it,' she said now, 'so Buddy actually believes he's saved the cat's life. But how?'

There was a lot to think about to make the

scheme work. The first thing they had to do was get Lola upstairs and into the closet without Buddy smelling the cat and causing an uproar. Antwan checked on him and came back to the kitchen.

'Guess what movie he's watching?' Antwan grinning. '*Buddy and the Kidnappers*. Honest. You don't believe me, go look. Buddy raised his head and sniffed, just once, and went back to watching himself on the screen, Buddy saving little Pedro from the bad guys.'

They got Lola upstairs before the family came home, but then had to worry about the kids, especially Courtney, coming into Miss Betty's room when Lola was out of the closet. 'We can't keep her in there all day,' Miss Betty said. 'I've heard cats can see in the dark. Still, the poor kitty could die of fright.'

Antwan's eyes brightened. 'If she does, better tell me right away so I can dispose of the remains.'

Miss Betty scolded him, saying, 'Think about making this work instead of worrying about your stomach for a change.' She said she'd keep her bedroom door closed; if she heard anyone in the hall she'd shoo Lola into the closet quick. The only one who might smell her was Buddy, but he hardly ever came in the room.

'I just thought of something,' Antwan said. 'What's she gonna eat?'

'Kibbles,' Miss Betty said, 'like everybody else. Or those meat-flavoured treats. Though she might not eat junk food.'

'Where'll she go to the bathroom?'

'Bring up some newspapers.'

'I heard cats use something else.'

'A litter box,' Miss Betty said, 'but we don't happen to have one. Go and get the newspapers while I talk to Lola and get her settled.'

So you're in kitty-cat shows, huh?'

'And you're the famous Miss Betty,' Lola said, looking at the display of trophies and photographs. 'Well, I've won way more than you. Sixteen red ribbons.'

'You mean,' Miss Betty said, 'you're the best-looking cat in the show? With that little pug face? You don't even have a *nose*. See mine? Nice and long and has that handsome black sniffer on the end? Honey, this is a *nose*.'

Lola gave a little shake to fluff her hair.

'My room's bigger than this one and it's prettier. They hang special draperies that I can claw all I want.'

'I bet you live alone,' Miss Betty said, 'don't know what to do with yourself.'

'I have my master. She kisses me on the mouth.'

'How's her breath?'

'Not too bad.'

'You ought to smell some of the breaths around here. I won't say which ones,' Miss Betty said. 'You kiss your master back to get what you want?'

'Of course,' Lola said.

'You ought to live with a German shepherd who thinks he runs the house. He did pay for it, but that's another story. His name's Buddy, and you know what? For some strange reason he loves cats. Don't ask me why. It might be old age or he's forgotten he's a dog. And now we have a boarder, Antwan. Thinks he's cool 'cause he's from the Hollywood Hills.' Miss Betty paused. 'He is, sort of, for a coyote.'

Lola jumped hearing the word 'coyote' and her legs stiffened. 'How can you have a coyote in the house?' A note of terror in her little cat voice. 'What's he doing here?'

'I find out,' Miss Betty said, 'I'll let you know.'

'Is he a friend of yours?'

'You'll have to wait on that one, too. Listen,' Miss Betty said, 'don't think about it, or worry what's gonna happen to you. If you don't make any noise or cause trouble, you'll be out of here in no time, back to that one who kisses you with the bad breath.'

Lola didn't understand.

That was all right, because now Miss Betty said, 'But if you try to run, or think if you cry loud enough you'll be rescued, it won't happen. The Hollywood Hills coyote I mentioned? He'll have you for dinner.'

Just at that moment Lola heard a sound coming from the hall.

She didn't think Miss Betty's big floppy ears under that ridiculous hairdo could have caught the sound.

But she did hear it, rushed Lola into the closet and pushed the door shut after her.

Only it didn't close all the way. Lola pressed her face to the opening where a crack of light showed from the bedroom. She saw a little girl giving Miss Betty tidbits from a plastic bag with a cartoon doggy on it.

And saw the bedroom door to the hall left open.

Should she make a run for it?

Not knowing where she was, or how to get out of the house?

No, first she had to think about what she was doing here. What if they were going to eat her? Or maybe it was something Lola and the other Persians had talked about at shows. Catnapping: humans grabbing you, hiding you someplace, and then they either let you go – like threw you out of a car – or you disappeared and no one ever saw you again.

It looked like that's what this was about. Maybe the coyote was trained to kidnap cats, and if he ever ate one they'd beat him. She hoped so.

Now she was wondering about the German shepherd who liked cats, Buddy, and if he was in the house somewhere.

She watched the little girl hold the tidbit over her head, making Miss Betty beg for it. Lola's master never did mean things like that. She called her Lolums and Sweetums.

The little girl walked out of the room.

Leaving the door open.

Miss Betty didn't notice it right away. When she did, she strolled over and pushed the door closed with that big black nose she was so proud of.

It told Lola this poodle didn't know much of anything about cats, especially how quick and crafty they were.

eight

timmy

Not the next morning but the one after, Buddy said to Antwan at breakfast, 'What've you been doing? I haven't seen you lately.'

'Same old,' Antwan said, his nose in the dish of fried eggs the maid fixed for him when he whimpered and gave her the look, with toast.

'Been hanging with Miss Betty, huh?'

Yes, he had, up in her room, but said to Buddy, 'I chase her around, pretend I want to bite off her pom-pom.'

'I used to do that. I think she likes it – acts scared so you'll keep chasing her. By the way,' Buddy said, 'you hear about the cat that disappeared?'

Antwan raised his nose from the dish, but then only said, 'Uh-unh,' not wanting to sound too interested.

'Yeah, the mom and dad were talking about it,' Buddy said. 'Yesterday some kids came to the door asking if anyone had seen her. They put up a poster along the road says she's missing and offers a reward to whoever finds her. It even has her picture on it.'

'What kind of cat is it?' Antwan said, acting interested now.

'A white Persian named Lola. They said she was in a movie, but I've never heard of any Lola. There was a Crissy in *Buddy to the Rescue,* the little girl's cat. When we can't find Crissy we know it was the wolves got her.'

'I saw the picture,' Antwan said, and asked then, 'What do you think happened to Lola?'

'Got bored and sneaked off,' Buddy said.

Antwan said, 'I wonder how she got out of there.' Saw Buddy lift his head to look at him and knew he'd made a mistake.

'Out of where?' Buddy said.

'The house where she lives.'

Buddy kept looking at him, working the taste of breakfast in his mouth. Now he said, 'You were gone the other day, weren't you?'

'Took a run in the woods.'

'You didn't happen to see her, did you, a white Persian?'

'I would've told you,' Antwan said.

Buddy didn't say if he believed that or not. He finished his breakfast and went outside.

Antwan went upstairs, the kids still in bed, and put his head against Miss Betty's door. With no lock on it the door was easy to push open. He saw her standing by the closet, but didn't say anything until he'd closed the door.

'They're looking for her.'

'It's what they do,' Miss Betty said.

'Homes thinks Lola took off by herself. I said how would she get out of there?'

Miss Betty frowned. 'Oh, no.'

'He knew I was gone for a while the other day, but didn't mention you. He asked if I happened to see Lola while I was out. I said to him, "I would've told you."'

'Well, he knows that isn't true,' Miss Betty said. 'He might suspect you ate Lola, but would never imagine you doing anything else with her.'

'How is she?'

Miss Betty moved away from the closet. 'I told her about Buddy, that he was a movie star –'

'She's in movies, too.'

'She was in a horror movie. I told her Buddy loved cats and now she keeps asking about him.'

Miss Betty putting on a tiny little kitty voice to say, '"Why can't I meet him?" I told her she would if she promised to be good and not act up.'

Antwan went over to the closet. He said, 'It's not shut all the way.'

'It sticks,' Miss Betty said. 'I put the latch between my teeth to pull it open.'

Antwan placed his nose against the edge of the door and sniffed. He could tell Lola was there in the dark without seeing her. He said, 'Hey, Lola? You smell good enough to eat.'

Lola saw the coyote's nose filling the space and heard his voice. Now the nose turned away and was gone. She crept over to the slit of light, put her pug face against it and watched Antwan walk to the bedroom door and work it open with his nose. There was something on the floor to stop the door from closing all the way – it looked like a block of wood – otherwise Miss Poodle wouldn't be able to get out.

He had the door open enough to slip through – Lola waiting to see if the poodle would come over and close it – when Miss Betty called to the coyote.

'Would you lend me your nose for a minute?'

Dogs used their noses all the time, poking them at things, poking *her* now, Miss Poodle asking was she okay, was she comfortable. Lola used her dainty pink nose only to smell things. She couldn't imagine sticking it in places she didn't know about.

Lola, with hope in her heart, watched Antwan turn from the door. Leaving it open.

No, the cool Hollywood Hills coyote turned back again and closed it. Darn it.

Now he went over to Miss Helpless Poodle standing by the window saying she'd like some fresh air. Like the door, the window was held open by a small block of wood.

Lola watched them hunch down to stick their noses into the narrow opening, watched them both raise up at the same time and the window came with them.

She heard Miss Poodle say, 'Ah, that's better.' The two of them leaning on the windowsill now, looking out at the yard.

Buddy was walking toward the house. He looked up to see their faces in the window, Antwan and Miss Betty.

Now just Betty.

Antwan had backed away, not wanting to be seen. But why? Not because he was with Betty. Buddy knew for a fact Antwan was in and out of her room all day – Betty believing she was changing him, and Antwan didn't seem to mind it. No, it was something else.

And Buddy thought right away of Antwan saying at breakfast, 'I wonder how she got out of there.' The cat named Lola. It slipped out, as much as Antwan saying, 'I wonder how she got over that fence with the razor wire on top?' Buddy had heard the mom and dad talking about the house and the cat's owner, all that. And knew for certain Antwan hadn't heard a word of it. The coyote could only pick up a few human words. He might someday understand as much as Buddy.

Antwan knew where the cat lived. Buddy was sure of it.

Once this was in Buddy's mind – that Antwan and maybe even Betty had something to do with the cat – it stuck there and became fact until proved otherwise.

Buddy ran toward the dog door.

Miss Betty turned from the window.

'He's coming. You'd better get out of here, quick.'

'He saw me,' Antwan said. 'He's gonna come in here and smell her, you know that. But listen, maybe you can talk him into doing it anyway.'

'*Me?*' Miss Betty said. 'You're the talker.'

'Yeah, but it was your idea.'

Buddy came in just then, pushed in and stood there looking at them, leaving the door open.

He said to Antwan, 'How'd you get in the yard?'

Antwan gave Miss Betty a look and a shrug and turned back to Buddy. 'Over the house. It wasn't nothing.'

'You eat her there or in the woods?'

'I don't believe it,' Antwan said. 'Homes, you have something wrong with your nose?'

Buddy sniffed. Why he hadn't caught the scent the moment he walked in – his mind had been stuck on Antwan.

'You have her here.'

'Buddy, we have an idea that would be fun.' Miss Betty speaking now. 'You find Lola, you know, outside somewhere, and take her back to her owner.'

'Then what?'

'It's like we're pulling a trick on humans for a change,' Miss Betty said. 'It would be fun.'

'Who for, you or me?' He turned to Antwan. 'How did you keep from eating her?'

'It was hard,' Antwan said.

'Good. Don't change,' Buddy said. Then to Betty, 'Bring her out. Then you two leave. I want to talk to Lola alone.'

Buddy brought Lola over to the window so she could get some fresh air.

'Have they treated you all right?'

'If you think being locked up in the dark is all right,' Lola said. 'I don't.'

'Can't cats see in the dark?'

'If you want to believe that, go ahead.'

Lola looked over the sill to see the roof, just a short hop from the window.

'Are you hungry?'

'I had some doggy treats. I don't know how you can eat them.'

'I'll get you home soon, don't worry,' Buddy said.

'That's what Miss Poodle kept saying.'

'They were just playing around with you.'

'The coyote?'

'No, really, they're just playing a trick. Listen,' Buddy said, 'what I want to ask you, what movies you appeared in. I might've seen them.'

'Well, I did *The Return of the Slime Creatures* –'

'You worked for Harry Zimm?' Like *that* he was out of his serious mood. 'He produced all my movies, the Buddy series.'

'I knew Crissy, the Angora that was in the one with the wolves?'

'*Buddy to the Rescue*, the first one. It opened and Harry Zimm said to me, "Fella, I'm gonna make you rich."'

'I tested for *Slime Creatures*,' Lola said, 'and Harry picked me because of my pure white coat against all the green slime, the contrast. I played decorative parts in a few other pictures, always the human females' cat. They never stop stroking, even between takes.'

'You know the business,' Buddy said. 'Why'd you quit?'

'No work. Orientals are big now, some of them even look like cat androids, like that hairless sphynx you see in Austin Powers movies? My owner got me into shows so she can take credit when I win.' Lola blinked, sniffed and then said, 'I acted like a spoiled brat with Miss Hoity-Toity Poodle, and I shouldn't have. I even started it.'

'I know what you mean, though,' Buddy said. 'Betty's a show bitch and they're all the same. But I'll tell you, Betty's easier to live with since Antwan came to visit.'

'What on earth,' Lola the white Persian wanted to know, 'are you doing with a coyote in the house?'

'That's a long story. Maybe I'll tell you about it sometime.'

Lola said, 'On the way to my house?'

'If you want.'

'You promise you'll take me home?'

Buddy nodded. 'I promise.'

'Miss Poodle promised, too, only she's a kidnapper.'

'That's over with.'

'If I don't believe her,' Lola said, 'why should I believe you?'

'Honey,' Buddy said, 'you and I are different. We were in show business. It's like there's a bond between us and we know we can trust each other.'

'That's how I felt about Crissy,' Lola said, 'until I told her about a part I was sure of getting. That two-faced Angora played up to the director with her cute meows and he hired her instead of me.'

'Well, that can happen,' Buddy said.

'Yes, when you trust someone,' Lola said.

Here was Buddy trying to be nice and not getting anywhere. The best thing to do was quit talking and take her home. He said to Lola, 'Stay here, I'll be right back.'

He went out to the hall where Miss Betty and Antwan were waiting and told them, 'She's going home. Now. And I don't want to hear any more about it.'

Miss Betty said, 'Well, you are saving her, aren't you? Lola's owner won't know she was kidnapped, but I'll bet she'll give you a reward.'

'Like what,' Buddy said, 'cat treats? The sooner this is over, the better. Come on, help me sneak her out of the house.' He turned and pushed the bedroom door wide open and then stood there, not saying a word.

Miss Betty looked in and said, 'Where is she?'

'Uh-oh, the window, we left it open,' Antwan said. 'She must've jumped out on the roof.'

'Then to the ground,' Miss Betty said. 'It's high for her, but cats always land on their feet.'

Sure enough. From the window now they watched a white ball of fluff run across the yard, climb the fence, leap to the other side and disappear into the trees.

'She's a goner now for sure,' Antwan said, 'unless we find her before the brothers do.'

nine

Buddy didn't want Miss Betty to come, telling her, 'You'll mess up your hair and I'll get blamed for it.'

She came anyway, jumped the fence with Antwan and ran into the trees, Buddy yelling at her to go back home. Miss Betty did stop long enough to tell Buddy, 'Look, I've been in the woods before, so quit yelling at me.'

Now Buddy had to ask, 'When were you out here?' in a stern voice, like he was her father.

Antwan already had the cat's scent in his nose. He said to Buddy, 'I brought her here the other day, homes, while you're falling asleep watching your movies. She's cool in the wild, knows her way around. You want to stand here arguing? Or find the cat before some coyotes get hold of her?'

That ended the argument.

They put their noses to the ground and ran this way and that following the scent, sometimes in circles. It told Antwan this cat wasn't only scared, she didn't know where she was going. Hey, but Lola was brave just to come out here. You had to give her that. Antwan was thinking he ought to get to know cats more. Talk to 'em first.

They came to a hollow choked with brush and Antwan stopped to sniff and look it over. If she wasn't in there now she was a minute ago.

'Lola's in there,' Miss Betty said, always sure of herself, and started to work her way through the tangle of brush.

Right away Buddy was yelling at her, 'Don't go in there!'

Miss Betty stopped before she was too far in. She looked back saying, 'Don't you remember the story of Brer Rabbit, the part where he wants to get thrown in the thicket? It's a good place to hide.'

'It was a briar patch in the story,' Buddy called to her, 'just like this one. You're not a rabbit, Betty. You're not a cat, either. You're too big to go in there.'

Too late. She was already into the briar patch.

The next thing they heard from her was, 'Uh-oh.'

'I told you,' Buddy said, 'didn't I? Now you're caught by the thorns and all that prickly stuff.'

They heard her voice say, 'How do I get out?'

'Oh, now you want my advice,' Buddy said. 'Turn around and come out the way you went in.' He looked at Antwan. 'What should she do?'

'Learn never to go in places like that. You know what her coat's gonna look like when she comes out?'

'It's why I warned her,' Buddy said.

'And you're gonna catch the blame.' Antwan grinning at him now. ' 'Cause you old and wise to the ways of briar patches and such.'

They could hear her moving through the branches snagging her coat, and now she stepped out in the open, poor Miss Betty, covered with burrs and bits of leaves and things, stuck to her, topknot to tail.

'You have to get somebody,' Antwan said, 'to bite all those burrs off you, somebody more devoted to you than I am, 'cause they're prickly, cut your mouth up and swell your tongue. I did it one time only, for Ramona.'

'She's going home,' Buddy said to Antwan. 'Now.' Like he was too disappointed in Miss Betty to say it to her directly.

'You have some things on your floppy ears,' Antwan said. 'I can bite them off without hurting

86

myself.' He moved close to her and nipped at the vegetation. 'Girl, are you in pain or you just feel like a fool?'

'Go home.' Buddy telling it to her face now. 'They'll take one look at you and call the Caboose. Or put you in the car and go to the vet's.'

'She ain't hurt,' Antwan said.

'She was in the woods,' Buddy said. 'They'll want to know if she picked up anything.'

'Like what?'

'Ticks, parasites.'

'You serious?' Antwan said. 'Bite 'em off. Man, I'm in the woods all day long, I'm healthy.'

'You're different,' Buddy said. 'You're not anything like us.'

It got Antwan to say, 'But you think you can join the pack and be like me? Become a coyote?'

He waited, but Buddy didn't say any more about it. He sent Miss Betty on her way home, and now the dog and the coyote went sniffing after the cat.

Pretty soon the wind brought the tangy scent of coyotes, Antwan believing it must be the Diablos roaming the land. That way, across the slope and into those trees down there. He stretched his legs now and Buddy came bounding after him.

The coyotes were in a clearing where shafts of

sunlight came through the trees: six Howling Diablos in a loose circle, with Lola, back arched in her snowy coat, in the middle.

The first thing Antwan did was yip, 'Wassup,' and go around brushing noses, the coyote style of giving high fives. They asked Antwan what was up and he told them, 'Same old same old.' Now it was time to come to the point and he kept it simple. He said, 'This is Buddy, the movie star. Understand? Buddy from the Buddy movies. *Buddy and the Kidnappers*? We saw it every night it was playing at the drive-in. Saves this little dog name of Pedro from the bad guys. This is Buddy, and this is Buddy's cat, Lola. Understand what I'm saying to you? Buddy don't want you messing with his cat.'

He spoke to them this way when there was no time to explain and they'd have to take his word for whatever it was. And they would, they'd say cool, because Antwan was cool and always had a good reason for what he did.

The dog, the coyote and now the cat continued on toward the canyon where Lola lived. Antwan asked her if she knew the way. Lola seemed to think about it before saying, 'That way,' pointing her precious little face in the wrong direction.

Antwan said to Buddy, 'She don't even know where she lives.'

'How could I see where I was going,' Lola said, 'with you dragging me?'

They went on and before long Lola was lagging behind.

Antwan looked back to tell her, 'I'll take you by the collar if you want.'

Lola was sitting down now. She said, 'Just wait.'

'For what?'

She said, 'You'll be sorry.' Acting snippy now.

'I save her,' Antwan said, 'from being what's for dinner and she talks to me like that?'

'She's a movie star,' Buddy said.

He walked over to Lola and put his nose in her pug face as she stood up ready to run, but didn't move, held there by Buddy's size. He said to her, 'Honey, I saw your picture, the *Slime Creatures*? The contrast was there, your white fluff against the slime, but you know what? You weren't that good. Now tell Antwan what he's gonna be sorry about.'

Lola was timid now, Buddy's low growl having put her in her place. She said, 'I meant he'd have to be careful that he doesn't get shot.'

'Yeah, with Lola missing there'll be hunters out there with guns,' Buddy said, 'thinking a coyote might've got her. I've been listening for gunshots.'

'I heard one,' Antwan said, 'just a minute ago.'

Buddy said, 'Where's the house from here?'

'The next canyon over,' Antwan said. 'On the shady side this time of day. It looks like part of the rocks.'

'You've come far enough,' Buddy said to him. 'The hunters will shoot you on sight.'

Antwan believed it; he'd been shot at before. He said to Buddy, 'What about you? They'll think you're a wolf.'

'I was offered a wolf part once. I turned it down. They put that black stuff on your face so you look mean. Uh-unh,' Buddy said, 'I would never play a wolf. They're always bad guys.'

'The same way humans see us,' Antwan said. 'But you want to join the pack and become a coyote.'

'I'll give it a try,' Buddy said. 'It's hard to explain, but I think of coyotes having more fun than wolves.'

'We eat the same animals.'

'Yeah, but you don't eat humans.'

Antwan let that pass. And now both Antwan and Buddy raised their faces at the sound of a gunshot and its echo, far away. 'They sure like to fire their guns,' Antwan said. 'I wish I had one.'

He saw Buddy and Lola were ready to leave, Buddy saying, 'Don't worry, I'll get the little girl home.'

Antwan stood watching as they ran off, Buddy

loping through the brush, Lola scurrying after him.

It wasn't Lola Antwan was worried about.

Buddy was confident he'd find the way to Lola's house. They'd keep to high ground, look both ways crossing roads, listen for cars and the sounds of humans, and stay clear of houses dotting the hillsides. The only problem, Lola kept falling behind and Buddy would have to wait each time for her to catch up, her little pink tongue hanging out. He wouldn't scold, though, yell at the poor thing. No, he was patient and would ask if she was okay.

They stopped to rest in the shade of trees on a high ridge. Lola spied the canyon across the way and became excited, frisky, knowing she was almost home. Buddy poked her with his nose and she turned to him, her expression for a moment fearful.

'I didn't mean it when I said you weren't that good in the slime movie.'

'You hurt my feelings,' Lola said.

'You were acting like a spoiled brat,' Buddy said. 'I got mad and I shouldn't have. That part where the slime creatures grab you? I thought you played it beautifully.'

'I hated that scene. I end up in the slime pit.'

'But you fought hard, hissed and clawed at them. Really, you were great.'

'Well, thank you,' Lola said. 'Coming from a fellow actor it means a lot to me.'

'I was thinking,' Buddy said, 'I could come visit sometime if you like, talk about showbiz?'

'I'd like that very much,' Lola said, 'just don't bring the coyote. He makes me nervous.'

All they had to do now was make their way down the slope, cross the road, go up the canyon a little way and Lola would be home.

They were part of the way down, Lola so anxious she was keeping up with him, even getting a little ahead, when Buddy spotted the hunters: a line of them spread out across the slope. He knew that at any moment the hunters would spot Lola, snowy white against the dusty green of the brush.

'Keep going,' Buddy told her. 'Get out in the open where they can see you.'

Lola stopped. 'Are you coming?'

'I'm right behind you,' Buddy said, but cautious now, watching the line of hunters not a hundred yards away coming toward them. Now he heard shouts from the hunters and stopped in his tracks.

'There she is!'

'What's that after her?'

'It's a wolf – shoot it!'

The Pooch Caboose was in the drive, meaning Miss Betty was having her burrs removed. There was no way of telling how long she'd been in there. Antwan imagined the groomer biting off the burrs and saying 'Ouch' a lot.

He went into the kitchen for a drink of water. The dad came in and said something to the maid that had Buddy's name in it, sounding like he was asking if Buddy had come home. The maid said no, shaking her head. The dad started in on Antwan then, calling him Timmy and saying Buddy and Miss Betty's names. Now the dad was stroking Antwan and calling him fella. Antwan got tired of it, started to walk away and the dad said, 'Stay.' Antwan knew that one, so he had to stop and stand there like a fool, wait for the dad to let him go. The mom came in and the dad started on her, raising his voice like he was blaming her, but the mom let him talk, not saying a word. She went to the refrigerator and got herself a beverage. Antwan pushed through the dog door and went outside thinking about Buddy.

Buddy was the hero in movies so many times he believed there was nothing to it. But now this was real life and the gunshots were real, hunters out there in their suits – all different patterns of green and black, some tan. Cletus said they wore those suits so you couldn't see them. Antwan said that time, 'But if I know what colours the suits are I must've seen 'em.' Old Cletus said, 'Even if you couldn't you can smell the ketchup they had on their hamburgers.' Smell, man, was what kept you out of trouble. Buddy had it. Antwan hoped he was using it.

What was strange, here he was the first time in his life worrying about a dog.

The kids were on the patio now watching TV, Antwan still in the backyard when Buddy came over the fence. He looked the same, all dog, but serious and maybe tired from running. Courtney came over and talked to him for a minute and went back to the TV.

'What'd she say?'

'I'm gonna get it,' Buddy said. 'How's Betty?'

'Been in the Caboose since I got here. How you doing?'

Buddy looked up at the house and then at Antwan again.

'Lola saved my life.'

'Hey, come on,' Antwan said, 'cause he couldn't imagine it. 'That little bit of a thing?'

'We came on to hunters spread across the hill. I told Lola to go on, run down to them. The minute she did I hear them yelling at each other, "It's a wolf!" and now they're shooting at me. If I ran I'd have been in plain sight, so I got down behind some rocks. Now they had me pinned there and started up the hill to finish me off.'

Antwan couldn't wait, he wanted to know right now, 'How'd she save your life?'

'The little girl ran back to where I was, got up on the rocks and they had to stop shooting.'

'She must've got over being snippy,' Antwan said.

Buddy didn't like that. He told Antwan, 'Don't ever let me hear you make fun of Lola. She risked her life to save me.'

'Cool,' Antwan said. 'Then what happened?'

'The hunters came up holding their guns ready, like I might leap out at them. One of them looks at me and goes, "That ain't a wolf, that's

Buddy from the movies. See the red neckerchief?"'

'Good thing you still wear it. Then what happened?'

'I became a phoney hero. I must've saved her from wolves because they had wolves on their minds. Doesn't matter there aren't any wolves around here. One of them said it might've been coyotes after her. I wanted to tell him, "You're right, but I didn't save her." We had a group picture taken, Lola and me in front of all these hunters with their guns. Lola stood up with her paws on me, licked my face and everybody laughed – like at the end of a Buddy movie, someone asks do I want to go home and I bark.'

Antwan said, 'They must've taken you to the house then so Lola's owner could thank you and give you a kiss.'

'No kisses, but I got patted on the head some more and called fella. Some humans, that's all they can think to call you, fella. They like "boy" a lot, too.'

'The dad even called me fella,' Antwan said. 'Those people give you anything?'

'I told you, pats on the head.'

'That's all you got in the kidnapping movie, after you rescue little Pedro.'

'Because the whole point of the role I play,'

Buddy said, 'I don't expect anything, virtue being its own reward.'

'They say that in the movie?'

'My owner, the dad. Remember at the end how I'm getting all this attention and the reporters are talking to the dad? He says, "Buddy didn't rescue little Pedro to get his picture in the paper. Buddy only did what he had to do."'

'Yeah, well, it works okay in a movie,' Antwan said, 'but real life, man, that's different. I can imagine you thinking maybe a big steak, blood running out of it, wouldn't be too bad.'

'It sends the wrong message,' Buddy said. 'The pat on the head and the tidbit shoved in your mouth is okay. It's what we're used to. I wasn't a hero this time anyway, with Lola. It was a setup and I'd just as soon forget the whole thing.' He looked toward the house. 'I might as well go inside and let the dad yell at me, get that over with.'

'Wait,' Antwan said, his ears standing up, hearing a voice from inside the house. 'He's talking loud to somebody right now.'

It wasn't a minute later the dog door pushed open and Antwan frowned saying, 'Who's this?'

'Betty?' Buddy said, sounding like he wasn't sure. Then, 'It is, it's Betty.'

A Miss Betty that Antwan had never seen before. Her thick mane of creamy hair gone, her topknot gone, her puffs and pom-poms, Miss Betty shorn down to a short coat covering her, all of her show decorations gone, zipped off.

'You're a *dog*!' Antwan said to her.

Meaning it as a compliment, Miss Betty now looking like she was supposed to, what she *was*, instead of like a wedding cake with a black nose on it.

'You're a regular dog.'

Miss Betty looked at him with a terribly sad expression and ran back in the house.

'I haven't seen her like that,' Buddy said, 'since she was a pup. Why don't you talk to her, tell her she looks great.'

'I did,' Antwan said.

'I know what you meant,' Buddy said, 'but she needs something more than just being called a dog. She likes you. See what you can do while I go in and get yelled at.'

Miss Betty was sitting in her room by the window, looking out, staring like she was lost in thought, her back to her trophies, not even looking around when Antwan came in.

He didn't bother with the door, he went over to her and said to the back of her head, 'I have to ask you, don't you think you look fine with your new sleek and swift look?'

No answer – playing that game with him again.

He said, 'Come over here with me.' She didn't move. Antwan took her ear gently in his teeth and brought Miss Betty over to a pink oval mirror on a stand and placed her six feet away from it.

He said, 'Look at yourself. Go on, do it.' Antwan nipped the back of her head, raising it, and she stared at her glum expression in the mirror. 'Okay, now say to the mirror, "You looking at me?" I'm kidding. Say to the mirror, "Girl, you look fine."'

She hesitated. He nipped the back of her curly, crew-cut head, and she said, 'I can't.'

'Turn sideways. Go on, you got nothing to lose.'

She did it, she turned.

'A little more . . . There. Now look over your shoulder at the mirror and say, "Girl, you are a cool chick."'

'I can't.'

'Cock your hip a little bit. You know what I'm saying? You're cool and you know it . . . That's it. All right, now say the line.'

'I can't.'

'There's nothing to saying it. Look in the mirror and say it like being cool is no big deal.'

'You are a cool chick,' Miss Betty said.

'You sure? You don't sound it. And you forgot "Girl".'

99

'Girl, you are a cool chick.'

'You're almost there. But now you have to slow it down. Know what I'm saying? Put some funk in it, drag it, like you're listening to hip-hop in your head and you're on the beat.'

Miss Betty said, 'Girl?' and paused. 'You are a coool chick, you know it? Yeah, I know it.'

'You got it nailed,' Antwan said. 'Tell yourself that every four hours and call me in the morning.'

Miss Betty's gaze followed him out the door before returning to the mirror.

The next day the group photo of Buddy, Lola and the hunters appeared on page three of the *Los Angeles Times*.

The headline said: LIFE IMITATES ART. And below that: 'Star of the Buddy Series Saves Champion Show Cat from Pack of Coyotes.'

The dad read the entire story aloud, saying now and again, 'Listen to this, fella.' Buddy listened and walked away with his head hanging. The dad said, 'What's the matter with our boy?'

Antwan wondered the same thing. He said to Buddy, 'What's wrong with you, homes? Man, you're famous all over again. Have your picture in the paper –'

'Yeah,' Buddy said, 'for something I didn't do.'

The German dog was as glum as Miss Betty

100

when she first looked at herself in the mirror. Antwan shook his head, trying to understand these dogs becoming depressed. They had everything handed to them. They didn't have a worry in the world. What was the problem?

Maybe, Antwan thought, they tried too hard to act like humans. Another way to look at it: their heads were so turned around they had trouble seeing they were dogs.

The day after the picture was in the paper, Buddy's agent stopped by with his shiny brown dachshund, here to take a meeting with the mom and dad. The maid brought refreshments to them on the patio.

Antwan had never seen a Hollywood agent before, so he walked past to have a look at this short dude in the suit of clothes. The dude was busy talking, but stopped as he saw Antwan. The dad said, 'That's our new dog, Timmy.'

The dude said, '*Tim*my? He looks a lot like a coyote. Has he ever been in pictures?'

Antwan caught the 'Timmy' part but didn't understand any of the rest of it. He saw Miss Betty watching from her window. Today she seemed to be doing better, less glum, but said she had no reason to come down. Antwan took that to mean she was still self-conscious about her new hairdo.

Now he strolled across the yard to join Buddy and the agent's shiny brown lowrider dachshund named Swifty. As Antwan came up to them Swifty said, 'You don't look like a Timmy to me. Bro, you look like some kind of wild thang.'

'And you look like about twenty pounds of baloney,' Antwan said. 'How you doing?'

Buddy said, 'That's enough. Let's go inside and have a treat.' They passed through the dog door and now they were standing around in the kitchen, Swifty's long skinny nose raised, sniffing.

He said, 'I'll have a peanut butter cookie instead of the treat. I smell 'em close by.'

Antwan said, 'But out of your reach, Shorty. Cookies aren't good for you, they give you the gas.'

Swifty turned to Buddy. 'Where'd you get this mutt, off the street?'

'Be careful what you say to Timmy,' Buddy said. 'You don't want to upset him.'

'I don't even know him,' Swifty said. 'We came here to talk about you.'

'What's the deal?'

'A Harry Zimm picture.'

'Bringing back the Buddy series?'

The hope in Buddy's eyes died as Swifty said, 'Bro, that was ages ago. This one is based on a science-fiction book. Harry hasn't read it yet, but there's a dog in it and he thought of you right away.'

Antwan said, 'When he saw Buddy's picture in the paper.'

'You're not in this,' Swifty said, 'this is between Buddy and me,' and turned to him again. 'The only thing Harry's worried about is if you've put on weight.'

'I'm the same as I was on the Buddy pictures. What's this one about, a maniac with a chain saw or a mutation, a giant cockroach or something?'

'What difference does it make?' Swifty said. 'There's a part in it for you.'

'How much?'

'Scale. Only what he has to pay.'

'Get another dog,' Buddy said.

'Come on, you know Harry Zimm, he's a tightwad, he's still got his bar mitzvah money.'

'I want what I got for the last Buddy picture.'

'You won't get it.'

'Wait a minute,' Antwan said to Buddy. 'This guy is your agent?'

'Well, my agent's dog, but he acts like an agent, he tells me what's going on.'

Antwan said, 'He works for you, homes. You don't work for him.'

Buddy said, 'I know that.'

'The way it should be,' Antwan said, 'he gets

103

you what you want or you get another agent.'

Swifty, trying to stand up to Antwan looking down at him, said, 'It doesn't work that way, especially not for dog parts. What you want to do, bro, is stay out of it.'

Antwan put his nose down to the dog agent's nose and said, 'Tell me where you live, my brother. I'll come over and we'll talk about it.'

Swifty looked at Buddy. He said, 'I don't need this. We get you the part and you don't take it, you'll never work in this town again,' and went out through the dog door.

Antwan hopped up on the table, said to Buddy, 'Just one,' and gobbled up a few peanut butter cookies, ground them in his jaw and swallowed. He turned around once and sat down on the table before saying, 'You let that little hot dog talk to you like that? I couldn't believe it.'

'He heard that somewhere, about my never working in this town again? Swifty wants to sound like he's in the movie business, so he picks up lines like that to use. But I'll tell you something,' Buddy said, 'if ever a dog could work as a Hollywood agent – I mean a real dog – it would have to be Swifty. He's okay. You just have to get used to him.'

'I didn't like his smell,' Antwan said.

'He can't help that,' Buddy said. 'Swifty gets his

smell from where he gets everything else, from his owner. It's how my real agent smells, so it's how Swifty smells.'

Antwan helped himself to another cookie as he thought of something. 'Is it true humans take on a different smell when they lie?'

'Yes, it's a fact,' Buddy said. 'They lie and you get a whiff of something rotten. Like you get when you stick your nose in a garbage can. You might've noticed I kept sniffing while I was talking to Swifty. It's a sure way to tell when he's lying.'

'It wasn't a bad smell,' Antwan said, 'but it hung in the air till he left.'

'There are things movie stars have to put up with,' Buddy said. 'Like agents.'

Antwan nodded, accepting Buddy's wisdom, and said, 'You think you'll do the movie?'

'I'll go listen to the mom and dad talking about it,' Buddy said, 'and let you know.'

Antwan went up to see how Miss Betty was doing. He caught her standing in front of the mirror looking over her shoulder.

'Why there's a cool chick,' Antwan said, 'if I ever saw one.'

'I'm more than cool,' Miss Betty said, still looking at herself in the mirror, 'I'm *cold*, not having any hair.'

'You have a nice creamy coat on you,' Antwan said, 'curly around your shoulders . . . Girl, you're looking fine. I mean it.' He said then, 'Buddy got a movie offer.'

'I know,' Miss Betty said. 'I saw you and Buddy down there with Swifty. I bet he put on his act and you got tough with him, told him off.'

'I got on the muscle just a bit.'

'You have to understand Swifty,' she said. 'If you don't take him seriously he's fun to watch.'

Antwan said, 'How'd you know about the job?'

'When you all went inside,' Miss Betty said, 'I slipped out on the roof, right down to the edge over the patio, and heard most of it. Buddy's agent made the offer and the dad didn't hesitate. Yes, indeed, Buddy will take the part. The mom said okay, meaning she went along.'

Antwan, curious about the mom, said, 'What does she do? The maid's always here working around, doing most of the cooking. What does the mom do all day?'

'It beats me,' Miss Betty said. 'I know she reads, she listens to music . . .'

Antwan said, 'She remind you of anyone?' He watched Miss Betty shake her head no and he said, 'She's just like *you*. She's a show mom.'

'You're trying to be cute now,' Miss Betty said. 'Anyway, they're already shooting the picture. If

106

Buddy's ready, he's on tomorrow. The dad goes, "He's ready, don't worry about that." Then the agent said, "Oh, and why don't you bring Timmy along."'

'Me?'

'You're Timmy, aren't you?'

'Why's he want me there?'

'That's a good question,' Miss Betty said, turning to the mirror again. 'You like my hair this way, huh?'

eleven

Early the next morning the dad drove them to the studio in his silver Cadillac sport-utility vehicle, Antwan and Buddy with their faces hanging out of opposite windows to catch the breeze. They had to wait at the main gate while the guard phoned to see if it was all right to let them in. He gave the dad a pass to put on the dashboard and directions to where they were shooting this morning, way out at the far end of the backlot.

They drove down a street between sound-stages as big as airplane hangars. They passed the fronts of buildings that were seen in movies but weren't real. Like the spooky-looking house up on a hill that Buddy pointed to and said, 'You know what movie that house was in?'

'*Psycho*,' Antwan said. 'It looks like a real house, but it's a lot smaller.'

'Because they only shot the outside of it,' Buddy said, 'from a distance.'

'I know there isn't any inside to it,' Antwan said. 'I've been up there.'

'You've been here before?' This coyote kept surprising him.

'I've been to most of the major studios.'

'How do you get in?'

'Under the fence or over it,' Antwan said. 'There's nothing to getting in a movie studio. We'd go in at night, me and a couple of Diablos. Nose around, check the trash behind the commissary. It's where movie people have their lunch.'

'I know what a commissary is,' Buddy said. 'Where I'm usually working, out on location, they bring the lunch to *us*.'

'We hang around a soundstage where they're shooting a scene,' Antwan said, 'and wait to see if any movie stars come out. I saw Denzel Washington one time getting in his car. I saw Ethan Hawke. Another time I saw Reese Witherspoon. You know who I mean?'

'Reese Witherspoon? I know a dog was in one of her pictures,' Buddy said. 'Where'd you see the movies they were in, at the drive-in?'

'Yeah, or looking in windows where TVs are

on. There any big stars in this movie you're in?'

'I asked Swifty,' Buddy said. 'He didn't know.'

'Or what your movie's about,' Antwan said. 'I heard Swifty say what's the difference, long as you have a part in it. But don't you have to know what kind of dog you're playing?'

'What's there to know? I do rescues in the Buddy movies and show how smart I am in the other ones. Like my owner comes home, I walk over and push the button for his phone messages and he says, "Good boy," or something he thinks is funny like, "I'm gonna get you a job, Bob." I was Bob in that movie.'

They came to house trailers and trucks as big as moving vans in the yard of an old farmhouse and a big red barn.

'Those ones unloading equipment from the trucks,' Buddy said, 'are the grips. They do all the heavy work. The ones setting up the lights are the gaffers.'

Antwan looked up at the sunny sky and said, 'What do you need lights for?'

'To shine on the actors so you see them good,' Buddy said. 'That group sitting around by the camera? One's the boss, the director, another one's the DP, the director of photography, and the rest of 'em are their helpers.'

'I guess it takes a lot of people,' Antwan said, 'to make a movie.'

'More than you'd ever think,' Buddy said. 'I can never figure out what they all do.'

The dad drove the big silver Cadillac SUV into a field they were using as a parking lot and they all got out. Antwan, seeing Buddy's agent and his dog coming over to meet them, said, 'Homes, you know what Swifty looks like? A fat little sausage with feet.'

Buddy said, 'I'm surprised he isn't wearing his sunglasses today.'

They watched the dad and Buddy's agent walk off toward the group by the camera.

'We're ready to go,' Swifty said to Buddy, 'soon as we get you made up.'

'As what?' Antwan said.

'He means get my hair brushed,' Buddy said. 'Come on.'

Swifty led the way to one of the trailers saying, 'Harry Zimm can't be here today but wanted us to remind you, don't wear your red bandana. He said be sure to have it taken off in make-up.'

'What're you talking about?' Buddy said. 'I always wear my bandana, I'm known for it. We're still making a nice income on Buddy Bandanas – the Badge of a Hero. I don't wear it, I could be just another German shepherd.'

As they reached the make-up trailer Swifty said, 'It's not that kind of part. You'll see. Believe me, you won't want to wear it.' He turned to Antwan. 'Stay here, bro. You don't need anything done.'

Swifty went in the trailer with Buddy, and Antwan sat outside to wait, wondering what the little hot dog meant, telling him he didn't need anything done. Antwan thinking, Why would I? I'm not in the movie.

Pretty soon he wondered why it was taking so long to brush Buddy's hair.

Less than a minute later he saw why.

Buddy came out of the trailer with his hair going every which way. They didn't brush it in there, they mussed it up, made him look like he'd been in either a fight or a hurricane. Antwan asked him right away, 'Why'd they do that?'

'I guess it's some kind of action scene,' Buddy said.

He and Antwan both looked off to see one of the helpers coming toward them from the group. 'That's the AD, the assistant director,' Buddy said. 'Probably the only assistant on this low-budget shoot.'

The AD was saying now through a bullhorn, his voice real loud, 'Buddy, you're on, fella.'

'He could've just called to you,' Antwan said.

'ADs love their bullhorns,' Buddy said.

They watched this one stop now and look back at the group by the camera. 'The director's telling him something,' Buddy said. 'The one in the leather jacket and lavender scarf, that's the director.'

They watched the AD turn to them again and say through his bullhorn, 'Timmy, they want you, too, fella.'

Now they were near the group by the camera, everyone standing out of the way so the director in his leather jacket and lavender scarf could study Buddy and Antwan together. Swifty came over to tell Buddy to look scared, and the director said to Buddy's agent, 'Will you please get your mutt out of there?' Now the director was shaking his head as he studied Buddy.

'That's not the look I want.'

The director continued speaking to his crew and Buddy translated what he was saying to Antwan. 'My hair isn't the way he wants it. I'm not supposed to look like I was in a fight . . . I'm supposed to look like I've never been cared for since I was born. I'm homeless, a stray. I come to this farm . . . Now he's saying, "Where's Harry?" He ought to know Harry Zimm isn't here. You know, the producer. Now he's sending the AD off to the trailers.

The Harry he's talking about must be one of the actors.'

'The AD could call him from here,' Antwan said, 'with that bullhorn. It's so loud it makes your ears ring.'

'Our ears, yeah,' Buddy said, 'not theirs. Now the director's looking at *you*.'

'I see that.'

'Now me. He's saying, "What's he growling about? What's wrong with him?" Meaning me. Now the dad's telling the director nothing's wrong. He says I'm most likely just thinking about something.'

Antwan said, 'That what you're doing, fella?'

'Now the dad's telling him not to worry . . . He said, "When the camera rolls, Buddy will be on his mark."'

'What's your mark?'

'Where you're supposed to be when they're shooting. Now the director's asking the dad where you came from. The dad says I picked you up somewhere and brought you home. Now the director wants to know what kind of dog you are.' Buddy listened, getting the dad's answer before repeating it to Antwan. 'The dad goes, "You're not gonna believe this. I had our vet come look at him and he says Timmy could be a coyote." But the dad said to the vet, "Have you ever seen a coyote wearing a collar? Someone named him Timmy.'"

Now the director folded his arms and brought a finger up to stroke his chin as he studied Antwan and then Buddy.

He said to Buddy's agent, 'Yeah, Buddy's a police dog, definitely not a vagrant. He looks too well-fed.'

The agent said, 'I told you, didn't I?'

The dad said, 'I'm sure Timmy will accept the same deal you offered Buddy,' chuckling again.

The director said, 'Yeah, Timmy has that scrawny look I want. Like he's been scrounging all his life.' He said to the dad, 'You don't have any papers on him?'

'He must've run away some time ago,' the dad said, 'and has been living on his own. And you're absolutely right, he does have that scrawny look. Don'tcha, fella?'

Antwan poked Buddy. 'What're they saying?'

All Buddy told him was, 'He's calling you fella,' because Buddy didn't like what he was hearing: sounding as though they wanted to use Antwan in the part. But how could Antwan do it? He wasn't an actor.

The director of photography said, 'Here comes Harry. You could ask him what he thinks.'

'My boy,' the director said to the DP, 'the only actor you listen to is the one who sells tickets. In other words, the star whose name brings people to the theatre. He wants to do something that's not in the script, you say, "Hey, that's a terrific idea."'

The director raised his arm straight up to the actor coming toward them. 'Harry, it's great to see you, man. I was just telling my new DP, we couldn't make this picture without you. If you're ready we'll rehearse the scene, do a quick run-through before we light the set.'

The actor waved the walking cane he was carrying. He headed for the farmhouse now in his bib overalls and felt hat, the brim turned up all around, and stepped onto the porch.

Antwan watched him, trying to think of the actor's name. Harry something. Was in *Pretty in Pink*. Played Molly Ringwald's dad. Antwan remembered the name then and said to Buddy, 'Isn't that Harry Dean Stanton?'

Buddy, his head lowered, didn't answer.

'Look, will you?'

Buddy raised his head. 'Yeah, I guess so.'

Antwan squinted at him. 'What's wrong with you?'

Buddy didn't answer.

'You sick?'

'You could say that,' Buddy said.

Antwan watched Harry Dean Stanton sit down in a chair and tilt it against the wall, the walking cane across his lap. Antwan said to Buddy, 'I wish you'd tell me what's going on.'

'All right,' Buddy said, finally raising his head to look at Antwan. 'You're taking my place in the movie.'

For the first time since they'd met he saw fear in Antwan's eyes, Antwan saying, 'What're you talking about? I won't do it. I wouldn't even if I could, it's your part.'

'Look,' Buddy said, 'this happens to every actor. A time comes when you know your career is over and there's nothing you can do about it. You have to accept it without crying or making a fool of yourself. I'm out of the picture. If you don't play the part they'll get somebody else. My friend,' Buddy said, 'this is your chance to see if you can do something besides chase rabbits.' Buddy grinning now to show he was kidding. 'Take your Howling Diablos to the drive-in. They won't believe it.'

Buddy could see Antwan weakening, beginning to like the idea, even though he said, 'But I don't know how to act.'

'Don't kid yourself, you're a natural.' Buddy paused, the director talking again, and said to Antwan, 'He wants to know why we're growling at each other. Now he's asking the dad, "Will Timmy do what you tell him?" The dad goes, "Absolutely. He knows his commands."'

'As long as it's stay or sit,' Antwan said.

'The director wants to know if the dad can get you to slink. The dad has no idea how to do it but says, "Yes, of course." You heard it, uh? How they say *slink*? The dad tells you to slink toward the house, that's what you do. Go over to Harry Dean Stanton like you're scared to death but still want to be petted. You can do it, there isn't that much to acting.'

Buddy shut up so he could hear what the director was saying to the dad.

'Timmy approaches the house from the barn, where he's been hiding. The key to making the scene work, you understand, is how convincingly Timmy slinks up on Harry.'

'Did you hear it?' Buddy said. 'You slink.'

Antwan nosed around the cleanest barn he'd ever seen. No hay or horses, no interesting smells. You dummy, Antwan said to himself. It doesn't smell right 'cause it's a movie barn, not a real one.

He padded over to the dad standing in the big open doorway, the dad looking out at the film crew standing around in the yard with nothing to do. Antwan stepped outside and the dad said, 'Timmy? . . . Stay.'

The dad seemed to Antwan like a man with a simple mind. He threw 'stay' and 'sit' at you all the time, so you wouldn't forget who was boss. Antwan had stopped on the command. Now he thought, Don't make me sit. Please. He heard, 'Here, fella. That's a good fella' – one he knew from hanging with Buddy – and walked back to the barn.

'All you have to do is go across the yard to the house,' the dad said, sweeping his arm out and pointing. 'You know what I mean when I say *house*?' Pointing again. 'You go to house. There.'

Antwan had no idea what the dad was talking about. He didn't hear the word he was supposed to listen for.

But now he was beginning to catch a different smell as the dad said, 'I think you're gonna be a big movie star just like Buddy. You do this one right, producers will be breaking down the door to sign you up.'

It was the same smell that had clung to Swifty last night. The dad was lying.

Saying now, 'Harry will come out in the yard and play with you – you know, like he wants to keep you, give you a nice home.'

What was going on here? It sounded like the dad was telling him what to do, but at the same time lying. It didn't make sense.

Now the dad put both of his hands on Antwan's back and began telling him something. Antwan heard the word 'slink' – there it was, Antwan was sure of it – the dad pushing down with one hand as he said it and pointing to the house with the other.

The smell was gone, so what the dad was saying now must be true. He wanted Antwan to slink across the yard to the house. That's what the pointing was about. Well, he could do that, no problem. He could even give the dad a cool, coyote-style slink, belly almost brushing the ground, but decided to save it. Antwan hunched down about halfway, slunk a few steps out of the barn, and the dad freaked.

'I did it! I got you to understand me!'

He looked out at the yard, at the director telling something to his crew and the crew laughing.

'I did it!' the dad yelled. 'I got Timmy to slink!'

The director looked over. He said, 'Good for you. Is Timmy ready?'

'Ready,' the dad said.

'My AD will give you the cue.'

The dad hunched down close to Antwan. He said, 'Timmy, I know you can do it. I see you becoming a bigger star than Buddy ever was.'

Antwan sniffed. The smell was back.

The AD said through his bullhorn, 'Action!'

The dad gave Antwan a pat and a push, said, 'Slink,' and sent Antwan out into the yard.

Buddy stood with the crew watching Antwan come slinking out of the barn, almost crawling, like a coyote sneaking up on game. You can do that, Buddy said to himself. And felt his heart beating. He heard the director say, 'Beautiful. That, people, is how to slink. I can't believe Daddy got Timmy to do that.' He raised his voice then to say, 'Harry? . . . He comes almost to the porch before you go out to meet him. Right?'

The dude director in his leather jacket and lavender scarf was sipping from a plastic bottle of water now.

Buddy wondered why humans were so thirsty, almost everyone you saw carrying a bottle of water. He noticed Harry Dean standing now, leaning on the cane against his hip, and remembered Antwan saying, 'Isn't that Harry Dean Stanton?' Buddy realized now that instead of feeling sorry for himself he should've perked up and said, 'You bet it is. Watch him, the man is whatever part he plays. Like the white hunter in *Buddy on Safari*.'

But, can he scare a dog that's really a coyote?

Harry Dean was off the porch now.

Antwan was still slinking and – Buddy would

bet – getting that soulful look in his eyes. Buddy thinking, I'll never have to do that again, beg for treats.

He had made up his mind, he was through with humans. You couldn't trust them.

He saw Harry Dean holding the cane just below its curved handle, away from his side. Now he stepped out to meet Antwan slinking toward him. Harry Dean said, 'I told you to stay away from here. Now git!'

Buddy said, 'Uh-oh,' and saw it happen before he could do anything. Saw Antwan stand and shoot his tail straight out. Saw Harry Dean swing the cane at Antwan as he lunged, clamped his jaws on the bib overalls and Harry Dean stumbled, fell to the ground with Antwan on top of him, Antwan tearing the overalls apart with terrible snarls, Harry Dean yelling, 'Get him off me!'

The AD called through his bullhorn, 'Cut!'

And Buddy with the crew behind him ran out to save Harry Dean, Buddy shouting through Antwan's fierce snarls, 'Stop it! He wasn't trying to hit you!' Antwan looked up at him, confused, and now Buddy told him, 'Run – get out of here. I'll meet you on the hill, later.'

Without a word, Antwan took off to run through the make-believe streets of the studio.

*

Buddy watched Harry Dean standing now trying to hold his overalls together as the director came over and asked if he was okay. Buddy didn't see any scratches or bites on him. Harry Dean was calm saying, 'I thought Timmy was supposed to run when I yelled at him.'

'He *was*,' the director said, and gave the dad a dirty look.

The dad said, 'I don't know what came over him. Timmy's never done that before.'

'We become friends in the third act,' Harry Dean said, 'after he saves my life. Why don't we stay with Buddy? That's what he's known for, isn't it, saving lives?'

Buddy wanted to jump up and lick his face. But then remembered, he was through associating with humans.

'I'll work it out. Either get another dog,' the director said, 'or another writer.'

twelve

Buddy hopped out of the SUV and followed the dad to the patio where the mom was sitting with a cold beverage. Miss Betty left her side to join Buddy in the yard. They both listened as the dad said:

'Well. It was a complete disaster.'

'Whatever happened,' the mom said, 'and I have an idea what you're going to tell me, I can top it. How much do you want to bet?'

Here was the dad, ready to describe the disastrous scene at the studio, and he stopped, curious. 'What are you talking about?'

'For the past two weeks,' the mom said, 'we've had a coyote in the house. The vet called to say he reported Timmy to Animal Control. He took some hair samples when he was here and they tested positive. Timmy's a coyote. He probably ate the real Timmy to get that collar. You have to give him credit,' the mom said, 'he's a smart rascal.'

The dad could not accept this, even though he believed it must be true, having seen Timmy in action. He said, 'The dog would have to have been as large as . . . our Timmy to wear that size collar. And you think our Timmy ate him?'

The mom said, 'I think our Timmy can do anything he wants. And you know what else I think? I think Buddy and Betty and Timmy talk to each other.'

Buddy and Miss Betty immediately looked down at the ground and began sniffing around.

The dad put on an expression that meant he was being patient and understanding and said, 'Uh-huh, that's interesting. But would you mind if we stayed on the vet? He called Animal Control?'

'The fink,' Buddy said to Miss Betty.

'And they're coming over,' the mom said, 'soon. And I think he mentioned the police.'

'For what?'

'To pick up Timmy.'

Now the dad felt he was in control. He gestured to take in the yard. 'Do you see him anywhere? Did you see him get out of the Cadillac?'

'Don't overdo it,' the mom said. 'Something happened at the studio and he ran away?'

'Oh, now you have time to hear about it?'

'He ran away – yes or no?'

The dad hesitated before saying, 'Yes, he did.'

'That wasn't hard, was it?' the mom said.

Buddy and Miss Betty went out to the back part of the yard to discuss the situation. First, though, Miss Betty said, 'Did you hear her?'

'She listens to us,' Buddy said, 'trying to pick up what we're saying. She's even tried to trick me. We're outside, she goes, "You think it's going to rain?" And I looked up at the sky. She grinned at me and said, "Caught you, didn't I?" All I could do then was try to look dumb.'

'I know,' Miss Betty said. 'She seems to mention our talking to each other when she's relaxed, having one of those cold beverages. But did Antwan run away or what?'

Buddy described what happened and how he told Antwan he'd see him later.

'So he's okay,' Miss Betty said.

'He's fine.'

She sensed there was something else he wanted to tell her and asked, 'What is it? What's bothering you?' And had to prompt him again before he said, 'After Antwan left, Harry Dean Stanton said,

"Why don't we stay with Buddy?" He thinks I'm just right for the part.'

'You were in that safari picture together,' Miss Betty said, 'he knows your work. So you're back in?'

'It's up to the director,' Buddy said. 'But I don't care what he decides, the guy's a creep and I don't trust him. I'm out and I'm gonna stay out.'

'Not so fast,' Miss Betty said. 'You'd turn down the part because you don't like the director? You'd rather lie around the house, bored, watching your old movies?'

'No more of that,' Buddy said. 'I've talked Antwan into taking me up the hill to meet the pack. I'm turning coyote as quick as I can.'

What was Miss Betty to say, please don't? Knowing it wouldn't do any good? She said it anyway, 'Please don't,' and then tried an argument. 'What if you can't cut it? What if you can cut it, but they don't like you? They don't care for your old-dog attitude?'

'You sound like Antwan,' Buddy said. 'He's agreed to take me up to the pack, but says there's no way I'll ever make it as a coyote.'

Miss Betty said, 'Well?'

'I'm gonna show him he's wrong.'

There were tears in Miss Betty's big dark eyes as

she said, 'Buddy, you don't know how to live in the wild, you're in show business.'

He gave her a knowing smile. 'That's why I believe I can pull it off, become one of them. I'm through with humans. You know what they'll do now, don't you? Get a posse together and go after Antwan.'

He paused, looking into Miss Betty's sorrowful eyes. 'Honey, if I don't find him in time, they'll hunt Antwan down and kill him.'

'They kept a coyote in the house? Living with them? With little children? I don't believe it.'

Most people didn't at first. But now the story was all over the Hollywood Hills and neighbours were calling and coming over to find out if it was true.

'Timmy was with us a couple of weeks,' the dad said. 'We were positive he was some kind of dog. He never gave us any trouble.'

'Timmy loved peanut butter cookies,' the mom said. 'He'd hop right up on the kitchen table and wag his tail.'

Neighbours began saying, 'I guess it's possible.' There were all kinds of stories about coyotes living at least *close* to people.

'We had one had dug under our garage and was living there, with pups.'

'They know when the trash is picked up, so they come the night before, hang out in the bushes.'

'That's a fact, they watch us take the trash out, like we're waiters serving them their dinner.'

No one believed Timmy had carried off Buddy; the German shepherd was bigger than the coyote. 'And he's a tough old fella,' the dad said.

But there were plenty of stories about coyotes carrying off small dogs and precious cats, even a cockatoo. 'Climbed up to the balcony of our condo and snatched Kathy right off her perch.'

'I was walking Lotus, our little Lhasa apso, on a leash. A coyote came along and carried off my baby.'

'Blow air horns at 'em. Spray 'em with a hose. If I had a gun I'd shoot 'em.'

And there were those who said, 'Coyotes have as much right to the planet as we do. We have to learn how to live together.'

'You wouldn't say that if your cat got eaten by one.'

Animal Control called hunters and they came to the house in their pickup trucks: experienced hunters with gun dogs, traps and lures, ready to go after this varmint that had sneaked into a house. 'People feeding 'em is the problem,' a hunter said. 'Did you feed this Timmy?'

'Of course,' the dad said, 'he was part of the family.'

'You feed 'em they keep coming back,' the hunter said.

'Timmy was *living* with us,' the dad said.

'Don't worry,' the hunter said, 'we'll get him, nail his hide to your garage door.'

The mom said that wouldn't be necessary.

thirteen

Antwan and Buddy came out of the deep ravine where it opened up near the crest of the hill. They stopped and looked way down at the house and the humans in the yard.

'Already coming after us,' Antwan said. 'You don't stay close to me, homes, they'll run you down for sure.' He turned to see Buddy panting, his tongue hanging out, and said, 'Homes, you look dog-tired.'

Buddy would be middle-aged if he were human. This running uphill behind Antwan had worn him out. He told himself he'd get used to it once he was in shape again. He hadn't worked this hard since his moviemaking days.

'You can't tell where the dens are,' Antwan said, 'but the pack lives all around here.'

'I know,' Buddy said, 'I can smell them.'

Pretty soon he was facing them, coyotes coming out of the rocks and down from the higher ground, the pack looking him over with cold coyote eyes, coming closer to form part of a circle around him.

'The big grey one,' Antwan said in a low voice, 'is Cletus, our leader, numero uno. Show him some respect, he might not eat you right away.'

Cletus came to within a few feet of Buddy standing his ground, keeping his eyes on the pack leader as the other coyotes moved in closer.

Antwan said to Cletus, 'Chief, this dude is called Buddy. He wants to pass, thinks he can run with us.'

'He does, huh?' Cletus said. 'He looks to me like somebody's pet doggy, chews rubber bones and plays with pussycats.'

A coyote with a scar across his nose rushed in from the side to nip at Buddy's rump. Too late. Buddy came around to clamp his jaws on the coyote's throat and toss him yelping into the brush.

Another coyote, a female, ran at him, and Buddy stopped her nose to nose. She snarled and he gave her his killer growl and a glare of canine teeth. They were eye to eye as Antwan said, 'Ramona, behave yourself, girl. This is my friend Buddy I told you about.' He turned to Cletus.

'Chief, how about if we give Buddy a few days, see if he can keep up with us.' Antwan had the feeling Cletus would just as soon not take on this big German dog but would if he had to. Antwan said, 'I don't see none of the Diablos around,' to take Cletus's mind off Buddy.

'They went down to the junkyard,' Cletus said, 'mess with those outcast dogs down there.'

'The Howling Diablos know how to rumble,' Antwan said and turned to Buddy. 'Come on, let's have some fun.'

They topped the crest of the hill and started down through the brush on the other side. But now Antwan looked back and said, 'I knew it.' He stopped and yelled at the coyote following them, 'Ramona, you aren't coming. Hear? Go on back.' Buddy recognized her, the one who'd gone nose to nose with him. He heard Antwan say, 'Ramona's the one tried to bite you and you stared her down. She shows off like that 'cause she wants to be in my gang and I won't let her. She's my little sister and I don't want her chewing more than she can swallow. Understand what I'm saying?'

They watched Ramona, her head down, go back over the crest of the hill. 'Wait and see,'

Antwan said, 'I bet you a big rat she still follows us. Ramona likes to feel her heart beating.'

At the bottom of the hill they came out of the trees to a busy street and Antwan said, 'We cross here.'

Buddy said, 'But how?' because cars were whizzing by in both directions.

'Homes,' Antwan said, 'you telling me you never crossed a street by yourself?'

'It's been my job to keep the children on the kerb,' Buddy said, 'till the light changes.'

'Ain't no light here,' Antwan said. 'Just look out for the ones trying to hit you. There's a nice-looking blonde-haired female human lives around here – any time she sees me she tries to run me down.' He said, 'Okay, here we go.'

They ran into the street to start a racket of horns blowing, brakes screeching, got to the other side and Antwan said to Buddy, whose tongue was hanging out, 'That wasn't too bad, was it?'

Buddy was amazed at how quick Antwan was to spot humans and stay out of sight, ducking behind parked cars, dodging around corners and down alleys lined with Dumpsters, the hot scent of garbage filling the air.

'Smells good, huh?' Antwan said. 'But no way to get at the grub 'less they leave the trash bin open.'

They ran down another alley, slipped past a big truck parked in the way, and there it was behind a ten-foot fence:

JOE'S SALVAGE YARD

A field of old worn-out cars and wrecks sitting in the weeds, and piles of what used to be cars before they were pushed into the crushing machine and flattened.

KA-CHUNG!

Buddy jumped at the sound ringing through the yard. He saw the crusher now, an ugly iron monster with spotlights for eyes, a giant jaw that came down to crush whatever was shoved in its mouth.

KA-CHUNG!

'Eats cars, homes, like we eat mice,' Antwan said, 'in one gulp. Come on, there's my gang.'

They were down a ways along the fence, a half dozen Howling Diablos facing as many junkyard dogs through the fence wire, snarling at each other.

'That ugly pit bull's their number one,' Antwan said.

The others were mangy mixed breeds showing their ribs. A couple of toy-sized dogs seemed the most annoyed, acting tough, their tiny voices yipping at the coyotes.

'Like visiting the zoo,' Antwan said.

Now the pit bull spotted Buddy.

'What're you doing with those hyenas? Come on over where you belong.'

'He's got too much class for your crowd,' Antwan told the pit bull. 'Buddy ain't ugly enough to be with you.'

One of the coyotes sang through the wire, 'You ain't nothing but hound dogs, crying all the time.'

Another one said, 'They ain't never caught a rabbit and they ain't no friends of mine.'

And the coyotes howled.

Buddy watched them moving around a bit, feeling good and having fun. The next thing, hearing a howl from down the alley, Buddy and all of them looked in that direction.

Ramona was up on top of the truck parked by the fence.

'Showing off,' Antwan said, and called to her, 'Ramona, come on down. You hear?'

Ramona gave another howl, crouched, and now they watched her leap into space to sail over the fence and into the junkyard.

All Buddy had to see was that mangy pack going for Ramona and he was back in the movies. He was 'Buddy to the Rescue' again, running, bounding from the alley to the truck and into the yard, the way he had leaped from boulder to boulder, to save the little girl from the wolves. He could even hear the music from that movie again.

Now Antwan and the Diablos were leaping up on the truck to sail over the fence, chasing after Buddy chasing the mangy junkyard dogs.

The pit bull turned to face Buddy and fight – what pit bulls loved to do more than anything, when they weren't biting little kids. Buddy flew into him, knocked him down, got the bull's neck skin clamped in his jaw and shoved him howling into the open trunk of a Chevy.

Antwan jumped on the car to slam the lid closed. He said to Buddy, 'How you know how to do that?'

'The movies,' Buddy said. 'I took a wolf that way.'

Now the coyotes had the rest of the dog pack cornered.

But where was Ramona?

Antwan and the Diablos howled her name as Buddy raced in and out of the rows of cars that were waiting to be flattened, Buddy getting closer and closer to that awful KA-CHUNG of the crushing machine.

Now he saw Joe the Junkman come along in a forklift truck, slip the wide blade under a Honda, lift it and haul the car over to the crusher, its spotlight eyes watching, its big mouth waiting to bite.

Buddy's ears stood up at the sound of a howl, a faint one, followed by barks even fainter. Then KA-CHUNG and that clang rang in his ears. He watched the forklift coming back this way. Watched the blade scoop up a maroon Cadillac, the same kind the family once owned and he'd ride in it with his head out the window, in the rush of air.

He heard the faint howl again.

And saw Ramona in the Cadillac rising on the blade of the forklift. In the window – saw her face between raised paws scratching at the glass.

A door must've been open to let her in, Buddy decided, and the forklift jammed it closed picking up the car. He ran alongside the forklift now and barked. And barked and barked and barked. Joe the Junkman wouldn't even look at him. Buddy circled to get a good running start and leaped on top of the Cadillac to stand with his paws planted, looking at Joe looking back at him.

Joe yelling then, 'Get offa there or you're going in the crusher!'

Buddy stood on the hot metal roof and kept barking, eye to eye with the junkyard human, until finally the forklift stopped.

Joe, on the ground now, looked up to see Buddy

crouched above Ramona's face in the window. He said, 'Well, whyn't you tell me?'

And Buddy barked, 'I did, you dummy.'

Back with the pack again Buddy was a hero. The Diablos howled his praise, the pups came around to jump on him, and Ramona licked his face in appreciation.

'She likes you,' Antwan said to Buddy. 'Too bad you aren't a coyote.'

Buddy said right back, 'Too bad you aren't a French poodle,' pretty sure Antwan would know what he meant.

Cletus the pack leader said, 'So you're the Buddy who was in those Buddy movies. *Buddy Goes to War* and some others?'

'I was Buddy in every one of them,' Buddy said.

'They showed them at that drive-in theatre in the Valley,' Cletus said. 'We'd sit up on the hill and watch.'

Antwan got Buddy away from him saying, 'Chief, we're hungry from all that rumbling. Gonna go get us something to eat.'

He brought Buddy to his den in the side of the ravine, brush covering the opening in the wall of rock. 'It was a badger's den I made bigger

139

inside and fixed up,' Antwan said, 'laid in some carpeting.'

Buddy watched him nose into the den and come out holding a limp mouse by the tail. He dropped it in front of Buddy, who hadn't had a mouse in a long time.

'I forgot what they taste like.'

'Only one thing better,' Antwan said, and went into the hole to bring out a few more mice for Buddy.

Buddy looked down at the mice Antwan dropped in front of him, then walked up to the den saying, 'I'd like to see the inside.'

'Go ahead,' Antwan said, with a mouthful of mouse. 'Stick your head in there.'

Buddy parted the brush with his nose and looked in. He saw wall-to-wall rabbit fur, limp mice lying about, a scattering of all kinds of bones, big ones, little ones, and he saw a pile of what could only be . . .

'Cat collars!' Buddy howled.

A pile of them, and right away he thought of Lola the Persian.

Her collar wouldn't be here, but there were some that he recognized. Collars he had seen on Geeja and Suzanne, on Alex and Max, neighbourhood cats he had chased and played with. Cats as well-behaved as he was.

Buddy brought his head out of the hole to look at Antwan. 'I see you've had your share of cats.'

'Love 'em,' Antwan said, swallowing a mouse. 'I've never had a cat I didn't enjoy.'

'Some of them,' Buddy said, 'were friends of mine.'

Antwan, another mouse in his mouth, managed to say, 'Oh.' He swallowed and said, 'We like different food, that's all.'

'We're different in more ways than that,' Buddy said. 'I'm not cut out to be a coyote. My breeding won't allow it.'

'You showed you can run with us,' Antwan said, 'but if you feel you have to go back –'

Buddy nodded.

'Where I belong.' He said, 'I hope we can still be friends, though. Amigo, come visit us sometime,' and took off down the ravine.

Watching him, Antwan was thinking: Sometime? Or right now? He was sure Buddy's scent would raise the gun dogs and the hunters would find him soon enough. They'd bring Buddy home and all the humans would stand around rubbing his coat, telling him what a good dog he was, everybody busy with Buddy.

It would give Antwan the chance to circle around behind them to the yard, push through the dog door and into the house. He'd see how Miss Betty was doing and maybe score some peanut butter cookies. Antwan was still hungry.

The hunters picked up Buddy, snapped a leash to his collar and brought him home.

They were cheered and slapped on the shoulder and offered a cold beverage while Courtney and even Cody hugged Buddy and the dad roughed his coat saying, 'Hey, fella, where you been, huh? Out looking for Timmy? You have to stay away from him, fella, Timmy's a bad boy.' It was as though the dad still refused to admit Timmy was a coyote.

Buddy heard the hunters talking about going out again. 'Since we have the gun dogs here. We got den smokers and some good lures. One's the scream of a rabbit in deep doo-doo, about to get et by a snake or something.'

He saw the mom watching him, like she was waiting for her turn. As soon as the kids and the dad left him alone, the mom took Buddy by the leash and walked him away from the crowd. Now she stooped down to unsnap the leash from his collar and waited for him to give his coat a good shake. In a quiet voice then she said, 'Guess who phoned.'

Buddy turned to see her face close to his.

'You understand what I'm saying, don't you? It was your pal from the safari movie, Harry Dean Stanton. He said he was looking forward to working with you again.'

Buddy's tail began to wag.

'Harry Dean said he had a long talk with the producer. He said by the time they were finished the director was fired and you're back in the movie. Do you understand?'

His tail still wagging away, Buddy put his nose to the mom's face and gave it a few licks.

The mom smiled saying, 'You dog, you.'

She left him, and Buddy stretched out in the grass to rest. He watched friends and neighbours leave, waving to the mom and dad, who waved back going to the house, the dad saying, 'Let's see if it's on the news.' It was right after this that Buddy, once again the happiest dog on earth, raised his head and spotted Antwan:

Antwan slinking along close to the house. Now he was through the dog door, inside.

Miss Betty sat by the open window, her slim muzzle resting on the sill. She had watched the crowd gather in the yard, saw the hunters return with poor Buddy on a leash, saw the mom remove it and then look as though she was talking to him. Hmmmm – Miss Betty would ask him about it for sure. But first she'd say how glad she was he was home, how she already missed him . . .

But now she heard the faraway howl of a coyote and Buddy vanished from her mind.

Antwan, in the doorway to her bedroom, watched Miss Betty raise her head and seem to wait, like she was listening for the howl to come again. He didn't want to startle her. He said, 'Hey, showgirl?' in a quiet tone and saw her turn, her eyes shining, and he knew she was glad to see him.

She said, 'I wondered if it was you out there.'

'That howl? Girl, you hear my song you'll know for certain it's me.'

'You love to brag, don't you?'

'I only say what's true.'

'Buddy's here.'

'I know, I saw him.'

'Is he home for good?'

'I'm pretty sure.'

'What will you do now?'

'Me? Be a coyote, it's what I do.'

'But you don't have to. Didn't you like being a dog?'

'I was always hungry. I still am.'

'Lola's treats are in the closet.'

'I mean I'm hungry for game, real food, since you don't have any peanut butter cookies.'

Buddy was waiting in the hall, listening to them for a minute before coming into the room saying, 'That's why you're here, you're hungry?' at ease with Antwan and with himself.

'I shouldn't be running around in the woods just yet,' Antwan said. 'This is the safest place I know of.'

Miss Betty said to Buddy, 'I'm so glad you're home.'

'The old dog's come back a hero,' Antwan said, 'a real one. He saved Ramona from the crushing machine at the junkyard. It has to be a movie. *Buddy and the Jaws of Death*, starring Buddy in a true-life adventure.'

She turned to Buddy. 'What's he talking about?'

'Wait,' Buddy said, watching Antwan at the window now.

'You hear it?' Antwan said. 'There it is again.'

'Like a baby crying,' Miss Betty said.

They heard it again, the pitiful cry of a small animal in trouble, caught in a trap or in the coils of a snake, helpless.

'It's a rabbit,' Antwan said, feeling a rush of excitement, his heart already racing, his nose almost smelling the game.

'The hunters have lures,' Buddy said. 'They can imitate that sound and draw you into a trap.'

'It's a rabbit.'

And that was all Antwan said. In the next moments he was out the window, down the slanting roof to the ground, across the yard and over the fence, Miss Betty and Buddy watching him all the way.

She said, 'He *knows* the hunters are out there,' her tone filled with worry, tears coming to her eyes.

'Honey,' Buddy said, 'he's a coyote.'

'I know – but Antwan's different.'

Buddy said, 'You want me to tell you what I saw in his den?'

He waited. Miss Betty didn't answer. She rested her muzzle on the windowsill. Minutes passed. Now they heard a faraway sound that was like a crack of lightning and her head came up.

'A gunshot,' Buddy said.

Now three more shots echoed through the hills,

then silence. A long silence, time passing as they waited.

And then out of the dusk came the howl, the call of the coyote, the lonesome dog song rising to the sky.

'It's Antwan,' Miss Betty said.

Buddy said, 'It could be any coyote.'

'No, it's Antwan,' Miss Betty said. 'I know his howl.'

As the song faded she wondered if they would ever see him again.

ear intelligent reader

ou are cordially invited to a
marvellous comic extravaganza in
which solomon snow sets
ut to find his true parents.

rill at his
uest to
rack down
is silver
poon.

asp as our
ero triumphs
ver rogues and
agabonds...
ven though his
ots pinch and
's always raining.

The funniest novel in the world, ever!

Kaye Umansky

the silver spoon of solomon snow

arvel as he finds his destiny
but will it really mean wearing
urple velvet pantaloons?

nd out in
he silver spoon of solomon snow

The Gloriumptious World of Dahl

Also available on Puffin Audio

www.roalddahl.com